OEDIPUS THE KING

OEDIPUS
THE KING

Sophocles

Supplementary material written by Frederic Will
Series edited by Cynthia Brantley Johnson
Translated by Bernard Knox

POCKET BOOKS
NEW YORK LONDON TORONTO SYDNEY

This book is a work of fiction. Names, characters, places and incidents are products of the author's imagination or are used fictitiously. Any resemblance to actual events or locales or persons, living or dead, is entirely coincidental.

An *Original* Publication of POCKET BOOKS

 POCKET BOOKS, a division of Simon & Schuster, Inc.
1230 Avenue of the Americas, New York, NY 10020

Translation, Preface copyright copyright © 1959 by Bernard M.W. Knox
Copyright renewed © 1987 by Bernard M.W. Knox

Supplementary materials copyright © 2005 by Simon & Schuster, Inc.

ISBN-13: 978-1-4165-0033-9
ISBN-10:   1-4165-0033-2

This Pocket Books printing July 2005

10 9 8 7 6 5 4

POCKET and colophon are registered trademarks of Simon & Schuster, Inc.

Front cover illustration by Robert Hunt

Manufactured in the United States of America

For information regarding special discounts for bulk purchases, please contact Simon & Schuster Special Sales at 1-800-456-6798 or business@simonandschuster.com

CONTENTS

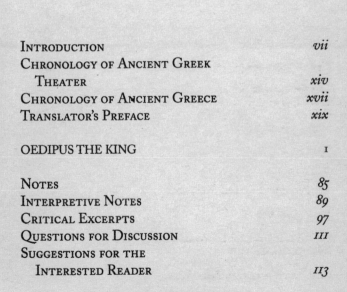

INTRODUCTION

Oedipus the King:
THE TRAGEDY OF FATE

In the world of Sophocles' *Oedipus the King,* everything happens on a grand scale, from feats of heroism to the most terrible of mistakes. It is a world of gods, prophets, kings, and plagues; a world of ancient tragedy whose stories unfold with relentless majesty and high emotion. As the great philosopher Aristotle explained in his *Poetics* (350 BC), the great tragedies are plays capable of arousing pity and fear, and thereby of purging those very emotions in us. Since at least Aristotle's time, *Oedipus the King* has been praised as a model of the greatness of Greek tragedy. For Aristotle the genius of the play resided in the organic perfection of its structure, and Sophocles' characterization—remarkably complex for his time—of Oedipus.

Generations of readers and spectators after Aristotle have agreed with his assessment of *Oedipus.* The king's flaws are clear enough to make his tragic fall believable, but so deeply enmeshed with his heroic qualities that we cannot help but feel sympathy for him. And while

some have found *Oedipus'* plot frustrating—the great
eighteenth-century satirist Voltaire complained that it
was absurd Oedipus knew so little about the death of
Laius—most readers have felt that its complex unfolding illustrates the mysterious nature and wondrous cer-
tainty of fate.

Beyond that point, however, the debates have never
ended. Some have argued that the play illustrates the
dignity of humanity. They see Oedipus as a wholly
noble human, pursuing his inquiry fearlessly and
accepting the terrible truths as they emerge. Others see
the way Oedipus' ignorance robs him of his heroism,
and argue that the play shows us the dark abyss of reality over which we skate through life, only rarely aware
of the cruel depths below.

These widely disparate views are typical examples of
the source of *Oedipus'* greatness: its mysterious polari-
ties, which are there for us to wonder at but never to
fully understand. The play gives us a hero who is both
nobly courageous and polluted, shows us that fate is
both cruel and grand, and that truth both sets you free
and destroys you. It reaches deeply into the mysterious,
noble, awful essence of human life and leaves its audience astonished and aghast.

The Life and Work of Sophocles

Sophocles was born in Colonus, a small suburb of
Athens, in 496 BC. His father was a wealthy merchant
(some scholars believe he was an armor-maker), and he
brought Sophocles up with all the advantages available
to him, including a thorough education in math, litera-
ture, and music. Sophocles rapidly became known for

his good looks and cultured ways. In 480, when he was sixteen, Sophocles was chosen to lead a choir of boys in a celebration of the Grecian victory at Salamis over the invading Persian navy. This event marked the beginning of Sophocles' public career in politics and cultural events.

In 468 BC, at the age of twenty-eight, Sophocles was invited to participate as a playwright in the City Dionysia, a festival held every year in the Theater of Dionysus for the presentation of new plays. This dramatic competition was the gateway to literary recognition in Athenian culture. Sophocles took first prize with his debut effort, defeating Aeschylus (525–456), who was then the preeminent playwright of Athens. This fabulous beginning was followed by an equally fabulous career in which Sophocles presented at least 120 plays, and won at least eighteen first prizes.

Throughout his life Sophocles maintained the cultural and political presence he had assumed as a young man. For many years he served as a priest in the cult of a local hero, Alcon, and of the Panhellenic god of healing, Asclepius. (This kind of service involved administration of the cult, and participation in public services in honor of the deity or hero.) He also served his city as a member of the Board of Generals, a standing committee devoted to the military affairs of the state. In this capacity he came to be closely acquainted with state leaders such as Pericles and the renowned historian Herodotus. For a time, in midcentury, Sophocles was director of the treasury for the Delian League, which was a defensive alliance among many of the major Greek city-states.

It is hard to assign exact dates to the productions of

Sophocles' plays, and even harder to pin down the details of his biography. Therefore we cannot talk confidently about the relation between his plays and his public (not to mention private) life at any given time. Scholars estimate that the first preserved play of Sophocles, *Ajax*, was composed between 451–444 BC, while his last remaining play, *Oedipus at Colonus*, was staged in 401, shortly after the his death. *Oedipus the King* was composed and staged around 429 BC.

Historical and Literary Context of *Oedipus the King*

The Rise of Athens and Greek Culture

The century that encloses Sophocles' long life (496–406 BC) saw dramatic ups and downs rivaled only, perhaps, by our own twentieth century. At the time of Sophocles' birth Athens was still a rustic and developing city-state; one among many such city-states throughout Greece that collectively forged a cultural identity during the fifth century BC. These early fifth-century city-states—Athens, Sparta, Thebes, Corinth—had roots in the epic past of the Homeric world described in *The Odyssey*, but were now beginning to awaken to the realities of modernity including a commercial economy, constitutional democracy (of a limited sort), and organized citywide cultural and religious events.

By the middle of the fifth century BC, when Sophocles was in his prime, Athens had proven itself the foremost Greek city-state. The great Persian empire had been defeated by the Athenians—a crucial military and cultural victory in which the outnumbered, but highly motivated, Athenians had defended their growing democracy from a monarchy led by despots like Darius and Xerxes. In the decades following Persia's defeat, Athens entered one of the world's most brilliant eras of civilization. The Greek historians Herodotus and Thucydides, who provided us with the stories and records of this midcentury outburst of political briliance and artistic genius, helped to establish our notion that the period from 495–429 BC was the perfection of this high period of Greek culture. The Western world's reverence for classical Greek culture is largely formed by our understanding of this era.

The Decline of Athens

By the later years of the meteoric fifth century, the Athenians had begun to fall apart. The greatest of Greek dramas—by Aeschylus, Sophocles, and Euripides—had become part of the people's experience, as had the construction of wonderful temples like the Parthenon, on the Acropolis. Furthermore, the city-state of Athens had effectively used its military and economic muscle to gain primacy over the many competing rival states of Greece. But overuse of this military muscle was proving too tempting to resist. In 439—to pick a typical instance—the subject residents of the island of Sámos tried breaking from Athens, and were slaughtered en masse. In 433 Athens formed a defensive alliance with Corcyra and thus initiated a policy of siding with certain Greek city-state allies against others. The internecine struggle against Sparta, which had earlier been the great ally of Athens in expelling the

Perians, broke out into the long-lasting (431–422) Peloponnesian War, which gave a nearly final knockout blow to the political supremacy of Athens. By the end of the century, thanks to some adventurist politics at sea and a reckless effort to intervene in the politics of Sicily, Athens had militarily been wiped out by Sparta and other rivals and had been superseded in all the finer productions of art and culture.

Ancient Greek Theater and the Cult of Dionysus

Ancient Greek religion does not bear much resemblance to modern monotheistic faiths. The Greeks worshiped many different gods and goddesses, most of whom, by today's religious standards, are distinctly ungodly—especially Dionysus. Dionysus was the god of human and agricultural fertility. Starting around 1200 BC, members of the cult of Dionysus began celebrating their favorite god with ritual orgies, multiday drinking binges, and ecstatic emotional, physical, and sexual rampages. For the ancient Greeks, reaching an altered mental state through these kinds of excesses was a way of releasing pent-up emotions and coming closer to the divine. By 600 BC, these religious rites were part of mainstream Greek culture, celebrated every spring.

In 534 BC, Athenian ruler Peisistratus added something new to the spring festival: a drama competition. At first, these dramas consisted mainly of odes sung by choruses of men dressed as satyrs—the lusty half-man, half-goat servants of Dionysus. During the fifth century, Greek drama became more complex, thanks to innovations by Aeschylus, Euripides, and Sophocles. The drama competitions of Sophocles' time drew enormous crowds, sometimes as many as seventeen thousand in a day, to open-air amphitheaters. These were not likely quiet, subdued audiences. Most would have been indulging in wine for days as a part of the Dionysian festival.

Sophocles' Innovations and Oedipus the King's Connection to History

Sophocles was a hands-on playwright profoundly immersed in the world of dramatic production. We know, for example, that he was an outstanding stage performer. Not only was he a serious actor, but the juggling act he presented in his play *The Nausicaa* was the talk of Greece for years. Eventually, Sophocles withdrew from acting, because his voice was not strong enough to reach the distant seats of the theater, but he continued to introduce radical innovations in dramaturgy. He is perhaps most famous for bringing a third actor onto the Grecian stage: Attic tragedy had sprung from a simple dialogue between the chorus and a single chorus leader, and even the great dramatist Aeschylus (525–456 BC), whose powerful plays formed the backdrop to Sophocles' achievements, had worked with only two characters at a time. While Aeschylus contented himself with characters—Agamemnon, Clytemnestra, Orestes—who were brilliant sketches rather than organic characters, Sophocles went much further toward rounding out the tragic character. About Oedipus, for instance, we know various mutually enriching traits: his pride, his hot temper, his remorseless intelligence, his capacity to grow through suffering. About Aeschylus' Agamemnon, we know only his mil tary determination and his headlong rush into tragedy. Sophocles also modified the Aeschylean practice of presenting his dramas in trilogy form. By compacting an entire dramatic concept into one play, instead of three, Sophocles made a decisive step toward the concentration of dramatic power.

Unlike the works of Euripides, a great fifth-century tragedian who wrote directly about the burning issues of his day, Sophocles' plays have a more indirect relation to their time and their creator's life. Nevertheless, the facts we do have can lead us toward fascinating discussions of the text. For example, Sophocles composed *Oedipus the King* around 429 BC, shortly after a great plague had assailed the city of Athens. Clearly, *Oedipus* is itself fundamentally concerned with plague and its pollutions. Whether it can be said to interpret the moral and spiritual meaning of such plagues, or simply to have incorporated their terrible resonance into the structure of traditional tragedy, is a matter for debate and discussion. Similarly, *Oedipus* was written while the cultural and political triumphs of Athens were still in place, but were just on the verge of beginning a precipitous decline, brought on, in part, by the arrogant overuse of power. Among the great and timeless issues Sophocles introduces to us—burning moral choice, the power of jealousy and revenge, the cruelties of fate, the dignity of noble survival—history brings its own kind of resonance.

Chronology of Ancient Greek Theater

---

534 BC: Peisistratus, ruler of Athens, institutes drama competitions at the annual Dionysian festival. First winner: Thespis, from whose name the word *thespian,* or actor, is derived.

496: Sophocles born at Colonus, a village near Athens. At this time, Greek drama consisted of a large chorus of about fifty men dressed as satyrs and a protagonist, who interacted with the chorus.

472: Aeschylus, considered the first playwright, revolutionizes Greek theater by introducing props, scenery, and additional actors to the traditional Greek drama. He wrote his first play, *Persians,* this year.

468: First victory of Sophocles in tragedy competition; he defeats Aeschylus.

458: Aeschylus' *Oresteia,* probably his last work, performed.

447: *Ajax* of Sophocles.

443–442: Sophocles elected financial manager of the Imperial Treasury of Athens.

442: *Antigone* of Sophocles.

440: Sophocles—along with Pericles—elected one of the ten generals of the city of Athens.

438: Euripides, *Alcestis;* probably his earliest extant work.

431: Euripides, *Medea.*

430s: Sophocles, *Women of Trachis.*

429?: Sophocles, *Oedipus the King.*

425: Aristophanes, *Acharnians.* His first extant play. Aristophanes is famous for his comedies.

423: *Clouds* of Aristophanes.

422: *Wasps* of Aristophanes.

421: *Peace* of Aristophanes.

420: Sophocles (a priest of Asclepius) receives members of the Asclepius cult on their arrival in Athens.

410s: *Electra* of Sophocles.

414: *Birds* of Aristophanes.

413: Sophocles elected city commissioner.

409: *Philoctetes* of Sophocles.

406: Sophocles dies.

401: Grandson of Sophocles produces *Oedipus at Colonus.*

317: Menander's *The Grouch. The Grouch* represents a style of comedy, many features of which are still popular: mistaken identity, farce, romance, and situational humor.

CHRONOLOGY OF ANCIENT GREECE

490 BC: Greeks defeat Persians at battle of Marathon.

480: Greeks defeat Persian fleet at battle of Salamis; Greeks defeat Persian army at Battle of Thermopylae.

478–476: Fortification of Athens.

477: Delian League, comprising Greek city-states and Aegean island states, formed with Athens as leader for mutual protection against future Persian hostility.

465: Revolt of Thásos.

462–460: Pericles rises to power in Athens.

461: Ostracism of Cimon.

458: Building of Long Walls of Athens.

457–456: Athenian conquest of Aegina.

454–453: Delian treasury transferred to Athens.

449: Beginning of construction of the Acropolis and Parthenon in Athens.

448: Peace with Persia. Sacred War.

446–445: Thirty Years' Peace between Athens and the Peloponnesians.

442: Ostracism of Thucydides.

439: Reduction of Sámos.

431: Outbreak of Peloponnesian War.

430: Onset of devastating plague in Athens.

428: Revolt of Mytilene.

429: Death of Pericles. Peloponnesians besiege Plataea.

421–420: Defensive alliance between Athens and Sparta.

418: Spartans defeat Athenians at the Battle of Mantinea.

413: Humiliating defeat of Athens at Syracuse.

412: Revolt of Athenian allies.

407: Battle of Mytilene.

405–404: Blockade of Athens.

404: Athens surrenders to Sparta. Long Walls pulled down.

TRANSLATOR'S PREFACE

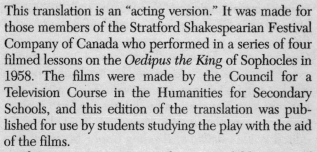

This translation is an "acting version." It was made for those members of the Stratford Shakespearian Festival Company of Canada who performed in a series of four filmed lessons on the *Oedipus the King* of Sophocles in 1958. The films were made by the Council for a Television Course in the Humanities for Secondary Schools, and this edition of the translation was published for use by students studying the play with the aid of the films.

There are now many translations available, some of them written with performance in mind. But when the films were made, none of the existing versions met the demands of the situation. The films, which were aimed at students in their junior year of high school, required a version that would be immediately intelligible, in performance, to an audience which had had no previous acquaintance with Greek tragedy and little acquaintance with the theater in any form. The translation has to be clear, simple, direct—its only aim the creation and maintenance of dramatic excitement. To put it another way, it had to be a version which would place no obstacles between the modern audience and the dramatic power of the play.

There was one version that seemed, at first glance, to meet our needs, one by a great poet, William Butler Yeats. He had made it for performance in the Abbey Theatre in Dublin, where it was produced in 1926. We actually began our work on the films using this text, but very soon realized that we would have to abandon it. In his superb versions of the choral odes, where Yeats used verse, he sometimes indulged his own poetic obsessions and produced images and phrases that have nothing to do with Sophocles—"the Delphic Sybil's trance," for example, or "For Death is all the fashion now, till even Death be dead." And though the prose of the dialogue scenes is strong and simple—"Lady Gregory and I," he wrote, "went through it all, altering every sentence that would not be intelligible on the Blasket Islands"—here, too, we were faced with a serious problem. For reasons he did not see fit to explain, Yeats cut the play in the same high-handed way he edited Wilde's *Ballad of Reading Gaol* ("My work gave me that privilege"); what the result is in the case of Wilde I leave to others to judge, but in the case of Sophocles it is close to disastrous. In the last scene of the play, for example, he has omitted 90 of the 226 lines Sophocles wrote, and he has moved parts of speeches as much as a hundred lines away from their true position, not to mention the fact that at one point he has taken two lines from Oedipus, given them to the chorus, and slapped them into the middle of one of Oedipus' long speeches at a point where an interruption destroys the power of the speech. As if this were not enough, he has, in an earlier scene, omitted Jocasta's famous lines on chance, without which the play loses a great deal of its meaning.

So the play had to be translated again. I have used prose (though in some of the choral odes, where the words seem to fall naturally into short lines, I have printed them in that form to suggest the liturgical style of the choral performance. I do not claim that they are verse). The criteria for the prose were clarity and vigor, and in the hope of attaining these two objectives, I have sacrificed everything else. The result is not Sophocles, but I hope that it will give some impression of one dimension of the Sophoclean masterpiece—its dramatic power.

Since 1958 many new translations of the play, in both prose and verse, have made their appearance and found their readers. But the Oedipus films are still widely used in schools and, in any case, the steady demand for this version of the play warrants its reissue in a revised edition.

The text of the play is complete; the few minor omissions of words or phrases are all dictated by the canons of speed and simplicity. In the first scene, for example, Oedipus addresses Creon as "son of Menoeceus." Few people in college, let alone high school, know who Menoeceus was, and the momentary check the strange name gives the audience cuts them off for a moment from the forward movement of the play in which they should be relentlessly involved. So I have dropped Menoeceus and translated simply "Creon." I have heard it argued that even though classical names may be unfamiliar to the modern audience they have a certain dignity and traditional familiarity which creates "atmosphere," but many years of teaching Greek tragedy in translation have convinced me that to the ordinary American student the name Menoeceus contains no more dignity than the name Lobengula, and is no more familiar; Lobengula in fact has the advantage in that he can pronounce it.

So in many other details. Apollo is sometimes called Loxias in Greek tragedy, and for the Greek poet and audience the use of one name rather than the other sometimes had a point, but actors cannot explain what the point is. In this translation Apollo is always Apollo. And the Delphic oracle is always the Delphic oracle, even if in the Greek it happens to be Pytho. Where the chorus speculates about "enmity between the Labdacids and the son of Polybus," I have translated "Laius and Oedipus." The translation aims to involve in the dramatic impetus of the play an audience which will find it hard enough to acquire even the necessary minimum of basic information. If we have to choose, and I think we do, between making students feel the excitement of the play and making sure they know who Labdacus was, I have no doubt which to choose.

The stage directions all envisage a modern production, not a reconstruction of the original performance. I have taken the liberty of adding a few remarks of a directorial nature where I thought them necessary to bring out the meaning of the passage. I have indicated my belief that the closing lines of the chorus are not part of the Sophoclean original, and at vv. 376–7 I have translated the manuscript reading, not the lines as emended by Brunck. My reasons for all this, and for many other things in the translation, will be found in my *Oedipus at Thebes* (Yale University Press, 1957).

I wish to thank Mr. Douglas Campbell, of the Stratford company, who gave me his expert (and overwhelming) advice on those parts of the translation which are used in the films, and an actress friend (who does not wish to be named) who went over every line of my text to test it for stage delivery. It is because of their patience and generosity that I have the confidence to call this translation an "acting version."

ANCIENT GREECE

OEDIPUS THE KING

THE CHARACTERS

in the order of their appearance

OEDIPUS, King of Thebes
A PRIEST of Zeus
CREON, brother of Jocasta
A CHORUS of Theban citizens
TIRESIAS, a blind prophet
JOCASTA, the queen, wife of Oedipus
A MESSENGER from Corinth
A SHEPHERD
A MESSENGER from inside the palace
ANTIGONE } daughters of Oedipus and Jocasta
ISMENE

*The background is the front wall of a building,
with a double door in the center. Steps lead down
from the door to stage level. In front of the steps,
in the center, a square stone altar.*

---

*[Enter from the side, a procession of priests and
citizens. They carry olive branches which have tufts of
wool tied on them. They lay these branches on the
altar, then sit on the ground in front of it.
The door opens. Enter Oedipus.[1]]*

OEDIPUS

My sons! Newest generation of this ancient city of
Thebes![2] Why are you here? Why are you seated there
at the altar, with these branches of supplication?

The city is filled with the smoke of burning incense,
with hymns to the healing god, with laments for the
dead. I did not think it right, my children, to hear

reports of this from others. Here I am, myself, world-famous Oedipus.

You, old man, speak up—you are the man to speak for the others. In what mood are you sitting there—in fear or resignation? You may count on me; I am ready to do anything to help. I would be insensitive to pain, if I felt no pity for my people seated here.

PRIEST

Oedipus, ruler of Thebes, you see us here at your altar, men of all ages—some not yet strong enough to fly far from the nest, others heavy with age, priests, of Zeus[3] in my case, and these are picked men from the city's youth. The rest of the Thebans, carrying boughs like us, are sitting in the market place, at the two temples of Athena,[4] and at the prophetic fire of Apollo near the river Ismenus.[5]

You can see for yourself—the city is like a ship rolling dangerously; it has lost the power to right itself and raise its head up out of the waves of death. Thebes is dying. There is a blight on the crops of the land, on the ranging herds of cattle, on the stillborn labor of our women. The fever-god swoops down on us, hateful plague, he hounds the city and empties the houses of Thebes. The black god of death[6] is made rich with wailing and funeral laments.

It is not because we regard you as equal to the gods that we sit here in supplication, these children and I; in our judgment you are first of men, both in the normal crises of human life and in relations with the gods.

You came to us once and liberated our city, you freed us from the tribute which we paid that cruel singer, the Sphinx.[7] You did this with no extra knowledge you got

from us, you had no training for the task, but, so it is
said and we believe, it was with divine support that you
restored our city to life. And now, Oedipus, power to
whom all men turn, we beg you, all of us here, in supplication—find some relief for us! Perhaps you have
heard some divine voice, or have knowledge from some
human source. You are a man of experience, the kind
whose plans result in effective action. Noblest of men,
we beg you, save this city. You must take thought for
your reputation. Thebes now calls you its savior
because of the energy you displayed once before. Let
us not remember your reign as a time when we stood
upright only to fall again. Set us firmly on our feet. You
brought us good fortune then, with favorable signs
from heaven—be now the equal of the man you were.
You are king; if you are to rule Thebes, you must have
an inhabited city, not a desert waste. A walled city or a
ship abandoned, without men living together inside it,
is nothing at all.

OEDIPUS

My children, I am filled with pity. I knew what you
were longing for when you came here. I know only too
well that you are all sick—but sick though you may be,
there is not one of you as sick as I. *Your* pain torments
each one of you, alone, by himself—by my spirit
within me mourns for the city, and myself, and all of
you. You see then, I was no dreamer you awoke from
sleep. I have wept many tears, as you must know, and
in my ceaseless reflection I have followed many paths
of thought. My search has found one way to treat our
disease—and I have acted already. I have sent Creon,[8]
my brother-in-law, to the prophetic oracle of Apollo,[9]

to find out by what action or speech, if any, I may rescue Thebes. I am anxious now when I count the days since he left; I wonder what he is doing. He has been away longer than one would expect, longer than he should be. But when he comes, at that moment I would be a vile object if I did not do whatever the god prescribes.

PRIEST

Just as you say these words, these men have signaled to me to announce Creon's arrival.

[Enter Creon, from side.]

OEDIPUS

[Turns to the altar] O King Apollo! May Creon bring us good fortune and rescue, bright as the expression I see on his face.

PRIEST

I guess that his news is joyful. For on his head is a crown of laurel in bloom.

OEDIPUS

No more guessing—soon we shall know. For he is near enough to hear us now.
[Raising his voice] Lord Creon, what statement do you bring us from the god Apollo?

CREON

Good news. For, as I see it, even things hard to bear, if they should turn out right in the end, would be good fortune.

OEDIPUS

What exactly did the god say? *Your* words inspire neither confidence nor fear.

CREON

If you wish to hear my report in the presence of these people [*Points to priests*] I am ready. Or shall we go inside?

OEDIPUS

Speak out, before all of us. The sorrows of my people here mean more to me than any fear I may have for my own life.

CREON

Very well. Here is what I was told by the god Apollo. He ordered us, in clear terms, to drive out the thing that defiles this land, which we, he says, have fed and cherished. We must not let it grow so far that it is beyond cure.

OEDIPUS

What is the nature of our misfortune? How are we to rid ourselves of it—by what rites?

CREON

Banishment—or repaying blood with blood. We must atone for a murder which brings this plague-storm on the city.

OEDIPUS

Whose murder? Who is the man whose death Apollo lays to our charge?

CREON

The ruler of this land, my lord, was called Laius. That was before *you* took the helm of state.

OEDIPUS

I know—at least I have heard so. I never saw the man.

CREON

It is to *his* death that Apollo's command clearly refers. We must punish those who killed him—whoever they may be.

OEDIPUS

But where on earth are they? The track of this ancient guilt is hard to detect; how shall we find it now?

CREON

Here in Thebes, Apollo said. What is searched for can be caught. What is neglected escapes.

OEDIPUS

Where did Laius meet his death? In his palace, in the countryside, or on some foreign soil?

CREON

He left Thebes to consult the oracle, so he announced. But he never returned to his home.

OEDIPUS

And no messenger came back? No fellow traveler who saw what happened?

CREON

No, they were all killed—except for one, who ran away in terror. But he could give no clear account of what he saw—except one thing.

OEDIPUS

And what was that? One thing might be the clue to knowledge of many more—if we could get even a slight basis for hope.

CREON

Laius was killed, he said, not by one man, but by a strong and numerous band of robbers.

OEDIPUS

But how could a *robber* reach such a pitch of daring—to kill a king? Unless there had been words—and money—passed between him and someone here in Thebes.

CREON

We thought of that, too. But the death of Laius left us helpless and leaderless in our trouble—

OEDIPUS

Trouble? What kind of trouble could be big enough to prevent a full investigation? Your *king* had been killed.

CREON

The Sphinx with her riddling songs forced us to give up the mystery and think about more urgent matters.

OEDIPUS

But I will begin afresh. I will bring it all to light. You have done well, Creon, and Apollo has, too, to show this solicitude for the murdered man. Now you will have *me* on your side, as is only right. I shall be the defender of Thebes, and Apollo's champion, too. I shall rid us of this pollution, not for the sake of a distant relative, but for my own sake. For whoever killed Laius might decide to raise his hand against me. So, acting on behalf of Laius, I benefit myself, too.

[*To priests*] Quickly, my children, as fast as you can, stand up from the steps and take these branches of supplication off the altar.

[*To guards*] One of you summon the people of Thebes here.

I shall leave nothing undone. With God's help we shall prove fortunate—or fall.

PRIEST

My sons, stand up. [*The priests rise.*] King Oedipus has volunteered to do what we came to ask. May Apollo, who sent the message from his oracle, come as our savior, and put an end to the plague.

[*The priests take the olive branches off the altar and exeunt to side. Oedipus goes back through the palace doors. Enter, from side, the chorus. They are fifteen dancers, representing old men. They stand for the people of Thebes, whom Oedipus has just summoned. They chant in unison the following lines, which, in the original Greek, make great use of solemn, traditional formulas of prayer to the gods.*]

CHORUS

Sweet message of Zeus! You have come from Apollo's golden temple to splendid Thebes, bringing us news. My fearful heart is stretched on the rack and shudders in terror.

Hail Apollo, Lord of Delos,[10] healer! I worship and revere you. What new form of atonement will you demand? Or will it be some ancient ceremony, repeated often as the seasons come round? Tell me, daughter of golden Hope, immortal Voice of Apollo.

First I call upon you, immortal Athena, daughter of Zeus. And on your sister Artemis,[11] the protector of this land, who sits in glory on her throne in the market place. And I call on far-shooting Apollo,[12] the archer. Trinity of Defenders against Death, appear to me! If ever in time past, when destruction threatened our city, you kept the flame of pain out of our borders, come now also.

There is no way to count the pains we suffer. All our people are sick. There is no sword of thought which will protect us. The fruits of our famous land do not ripen. Our women cannot ease their labor pains by giving birth. One after another you can see our people speed like winged birds, faster than irresistible fire, to the shore of evening, to death. The city is dying, the deaths cannot be counted. The children lie unburied, unmourned, spreading death. Wives and gray-haired mothers come from all over the city, wailing they come to the altar steps to pray for release from pain and sorrow. The hymn to the Healer flashes out, and with it, accompanied by flutes, the mourning for the dead. Golden daughter of Zeus, Athena, send help and bring us joy.

I pray that the raging War-god,[13] who now without shield and armor hems me in with shouting and burns me, I pray that he may turn back and leave the borders of this land. Let him go to the great sea gulf of the Western ocean or north to the Thracian coasts[14] which give no shelter from the sea. For now, what the night spares, he comes for by day.

Father Zeus, you that in majesty govern the blazing lightning, destroy him beneath your thunderbolt!

Apollo, king and protector! I pray for the arrows from your golden bow—let them be ranged on my side to help me. And with them the flaming torches of Artemis, with which she speeds along the Eastern mountains. And I invoke the god with the golden head-dress, who gave this land his name, wine-faced Dionysus,[15] who runs with the maddened girls—let him come to my side, shining with his blazing pine-torch, to fight the god who is without honor among all other gods.

[The chorus stays on stage. Enter Oedipus, from the palace doors. He addresses the chorus—the people of Thebes.]

OEDIPUS

You are praying. As for your prayers, if you are willing to hear and accept what I say now and so treat the disease, you will find rescue and relief from distress. I shall make a proclamation, speaking as one who has no connection with this affair, nor with the murder. Even if I had been here at the time, I could not have followed the track very far without some clue. As it is, I became a Theban citizen with you after it happened. So I now proclaim to all of you, citizens of Thebes: whoever among you knows by whose hand Laius son of Labdacus was killed, I order him to reveal the whole truth to me.

If he is afraid to speak up, I order him to speak even against himself, and so escape the indictment, for he will suffer no unpleasant consequence except exile; he can leave Thebes unharmed.

[Silence while Oedipus waits for a reply.]

Secondly, if anyone knows the identity of the murderer, and that he is a foreigner, from another land, let him speak up. I shall make it profitable for him, and he will have my gratitude, too.

[Pause.]

But if you keep silent—if someone among you refuses my offer, shielding some relative or friend, or himself—now, listen to what I intend to do in that case. That man, whoever he may be, I banish from this land where I sit on the throne and hold the power; no one shall take him in or speak to him. He is forbidden communion in prayers or offerings to the gods, or in holy water. Everyone is to expel him from their homes as if he were himself the source of infection which Apollo's oracle has just made known to me. That is how I fulfill my obligations as an ally to the god and to the murdered man. As for the murderer himself, I call down a curse on him, whether that unknown figure be one man or one among many. May he drag out an evil death-in-life in misery. And further, I pronounce a curse on myself if the murderer should, with my knowledge, share my house; in that case may I be subject to all the curses I have just called down on these people here. I order you all to obey these commands in full for my sake, for Apollo's sake, and for the sake of this land, withering away in famine, abandoned by heaven.

Even if this action had not been urged by the god, it was not proper for you to have left the matter unsolved—the death of a good man and a king. You should have investigated it. But now I am in command. I hold the office he once held, the wife who once was his is now mine, the mother of my children. Laius and I would be closely connected by children from the same wife, if his line had not met with disaster. But chance swooped down on his life. So I shall fight for him, as if he were my own father. I shall shrink from nothing in my search to find the murderer of Laius, of the royal line of Thebes, stretching back through Labdacus, Polydorus and Cadmus, to ancient Agenor.[16] On those who do not co-operate with these measures I call down this curse in the gods' name: let no crop grow out of the earth for them, their wives bear no children. Rather let them be destroyed by the present plague, or something even worse. But to you people of Thebes who approve of my action I say this: May justice be our ally and all the gods be with us forever!

CHORUS

[One member of the chorus speaks for them all.]

You have put me under a curse, King, and under the threat of that curse I shall make my statement. I did

not kill Laius and I am not in a position to say who did.
This search to find the murderer should have been
undertaken by Apollo who sent the message which
began it.

OEDIPUS

What you say is just. But to compel the gods to act
against their will—no man could do that.

CHORUS LEADER

Then let me make a second suggestion.

OEDIPUS

And a third, if you like—speak up.

CHORUS LEADER

The man who sees most eye to eye with Lord Apollo
is Tiresias[17] and from him you might learn most clearly
the truth for which you are searching.

OEDIPUS

I did not leave *that* undone either. I have already
sent for him, at Creon's suggestion. I have sent for him
twice, in fact, and have been wondering for some time
why he is not yet here.

CHORUS LEADER

Apart from what he will say, there is nothing but old,
faint rumors.

OEDIPUS

What were they? I want to examine every single
word.

CHORUS LEADER

Laius was killed, so they say, by some travelers.

OEDIPUS

I heard that, too. Where is the man who saw it?

CHORUS LEADER

If he has any trace of fear in him, he won't stand firm when he hears the curses you have called down on him.

OEDIPUS

If he didn't shrink from the action he won't be frightened by a word.

CHORUS LEADER

But here comes the one who will convict him. These men are bringing the holy prophet of the gods, the only man in whom truth is inborn.

[Enter Tiresias, from the side. He has a boy to lead him, and is accompanied by guards.]

OEDIPUS

Tiresias, you who understand all things—those which can be taught and those which may not be mentioned, things in the heavens and things which walk the earth! You cannot see, but you understand the city's distress, the disease from which it is suffering. You, my lord, are our shield against it, our savior, the only one we have. You may not have heard the news from the messengers. We sent to Apollo and he sent us back this answer: relief from this disease would come to us only if we discovered the identity of the murderers of Laius

and then either killed them or banished them from
Thebes. Do not begrudge us your knowledge—any
voice from the birds or any other way of prophecy you
have. Save yourself and this city, save me, from all the
infection caused by the dead man. We are in your
hands. And the noblest of labors is for a man to help his
fellow men with all he has and can do.

TIRESIAS

Wisdom is a dreadful thing when it brings no profit
to its possessor. I knew all this well, but forgot.
Otherwise I would never have come here.

OEDIPUS

What is the matter? Why this despairing mood?

TIRESIAS

Dismiss me, send me home. That will be the easiest
way for both of us to bear our burden.

OEDIPUS

What you propose is unlawful—and unfriendly to
this city which raised you. You are withholding information.

TIRESIAS

I do not see that your talking is to the point. And I
don't want the same thing to happen to me.

OEDIPUS

If you know something, in God's name, do not turn
your back on us. Look. All of us here, on our knees,
beseech you.

TIRESIAS

You are all ignorant. I will never reveal my dreadful secrets, or rather, yours.

OEDIPUS

What do you say? You know something? And will not speak? You intend to betray us, do you, and wreck the state?

TIRESIAS

I will not cause pain to myself or to you. Why do you question me? It is useless. You will get nothing from me.

OEDIPUS

You scoundrel! You would enrage a lifeless stone. Will nothing move you? Speak out and make an end of it.

TIRESIAS

You blame my temper, but you are not aware of one *you* live with. *Dramatic irony*

OEDIPUS

[*To chorus*] Who could control his anger listening to talk like this—these insults to Thebes?

TIRESIAS

What is to come will come, even if I shroud it in silence.

OEDIPUS

What is to come, *that* is what you are bound to tell *me*.

TIRESIAS

I will say no more. Do what you like—rage at me in the wildest anger you can muster.

OEDIPUS

I will. I am angry enough to speak out. I understand it all. Listen to me. I think that *you* helped to plan the murder of Laius—yes, and short of actually raising your hand against him you did it. If you weren't blind, I'd say that you alone struck him down.

TIRESIAS

Is that what you say? I charge you now to carry out the articles of the proclamation you made. From now on do not presume to speak to me or to any of these people. *You* are the murderer, *you* are the unholy defilement of this land.

OEDIPUS

Have you no shame? To start up such a story! Do you think you will get away with this?

TIRESIAS

Yes. The truth with all its strength is in me.

OEDIPUS

Who taught you this lesson? You didn't learn it from your prophet's trade.

TIRESIAS

You did. I was unwilling to speak but you drove me to it.

OEDIPUS

What was it you said? I want to understand it clearly.

TIRESIAS

Didn't you understand it the first time? Aren't you just trying to trip me up?

OEDIPUS

No, I did not grasp it fully. Repeat your statement.

TIRESIAS

I say that you are the murderer you are searching for.

OEDIPUS

Do you think you can say that twice and not pay for it?

TIRESIAS

Shall I say something more, to make you angrier still?

OEDIPUS

Say what you like. It will all be meaningless.

TIRESIAS

I say that without knowing it you are living in shameful intimacy with your nearest and dearest. You do not see the evil in which you live.

OEDIPUS

Do you think you can go on like this with impunity forever?

TIRESIAS

Yes, if the truth has power.

OEDIPUS

It has, except for you. You have no power or truth. You are blind, your ears and mind as well as eyes.

TIRESIAS

You are a pitiful figure. These reproaches you fling at me, all these people here will fling them at you—and before very long.

OEDIPUS

[Contemptuously] You live your life in one continuous night of darkness. Neither I nor any other man that can see would do you any harm.

TIRESIAS

It is not destiny that I should fall through you. Apollo is enough for that. It is *his* concern.

OEDIPUS

Was it Creon, or you, that invented this story?

TIRESIAS

It is not Creon who harms you—you harm yourself.

OEDIPUS

Wealth, absolute power, skill surpassing skill in the competition of life—what envy is your reward! For the sake of this power which Thebes entrusted to me—I did not ask for it—to win this power faithful Creon, my friend from the beginning, sneaks up on me treacherously, longing to drive me out. He sets this intriguing magician on me, a lying quack, keen sighted for what he can make, but blind in prophecy. *arrogance that derives from insecurity*

Tyranos [*To Tiresias*] Tell me, when were you a true prophet? When the Sphinx chanted her riddle here, did *you* come forward to speak the word that would liberate the people of this town? That riddle was not for anyone who came along to answer—it called for prophetic insight. But you didn't come forward, you offered no answer told you by the birds or the gods. No. *I* came, know-nothing Oedipus, *I* stopped the Sphinx. I answered the riddle with my own intelligence—the birds had nothing to teach me. And now you try to drive me out, you think you will stand beside Creon's throne. I tell you, you will pay in tears for this witch-hunting—you and Creon, the man that organized this conspiracy. If you weren't an old man, you would already have realized, in suffering, what your schemes lead to.

CHORUS LEADER

If we may make a suggestion—both his words and yours, Oedipus, seem to have been spoken in anger. This sort of talk is not what we need—what we must think of is how to solve the problem set by the god's oracle.

TIRESIAS

King though you are, you must treat me as your equal in one respect—the right to reply. That is a power which belongs to me, too. I am not your servant, but Apollo's. I am not inscribed on the records as a dependent of Creon, with no right to speak in person. I can speak, and here is what I have to say. You have mocked at my blindness, but you, who have eyes, cannot see the evil in which you stand; you cannot see where you are living, nor with whom you share your house. Do you even know who your parents are? Without knowing it, you are the enemy of your own flesh and blood, the dead below and the living here above. The double-edged curse of your mother and father, moving on dread feet, shall one day drive you from this land. You see straight now but then you will see darkness. You will scream aloud on that day; there is no place which shall not hear you, no part of Mount Cithaeron[18] here which will not ring in echo, on that day when you know the truth about your wedding, that evil harbor into which you sailed before a fair wind.

There is a multitude of other horrors which you do not even suspect, and they will equate you to yourself and to your own children. There! Now smear me and Creon with your accusations. There is no man alive whose ruin will be more pitiful than yours.

OEDIPUS

Enough! I won't listen to this sort of talk from you. Damn you! My curse on you! Get out of here, quickly. Away from this house, back to where you came from!

TIRESIAS

I would never have come here if you had not summoned me.

OEDIPUS

I didn't know that you were going to speak like a fool—or it would have been a long time before I summoned you to my palace.

TIRESIAS

I am what I am—a fool to you, so it seems, but the parents who brought you into the world thought me sensible enough. *[Tiresias turns to go.]*

OEDIPUS

Whom do you mean? Wait! Who is my father?

TIRESIAS

This present day will give you birth and death.

OEDIPUS

Everything you say is the same—riddles, obscurities.

TIRESIAS

Aren't you the best man alive at guessing riddles?

OEDIPUS

Insult me, go on—but that, you will find, is what makes me great.

TIRESIAS

Yet that good fortune was your destruction.

OEDIPUS

What does that matter, if I saved Thebes?

TIRESIAS

I will go, then. Boy, lead me away.

OEDIPUS

Yes, take him away. While you're here you are a hindrance, a nuisance; once out of the way you won't annoy me any more.

TIRESIAS

I am going. But first I will say what I came here to say. I have no fear of you. You cannot destroy me. Listen to me now. The man you are trying to find, with your threatening proclamations, the murderer of Laius, that man is here in Thebes. He is apparently an immigrant of foreign birth, but he will be revealed as a native-born Theban. He will take no pleasure in that revelation. Blind instead of seeing, beggar instead of rich, he will make his way to foreign soil, feeling his way with a stick. He will be revealed as brother and father of the children with whom he now lives, the son and husband of the woman who gave him birth, the murderer and marriage-partner of his father. Go think this out. And if you find that I am wrong, then say I have no skill in prophecy.

*[Exit Tiresias led by boy to side. Oedipus
goes back into the palace.]*

CHORUS

Who is the man denounced by the prophetic voice from Delphi's[19] cliffs—the man whose bloodstained hands committed a nameless crime? Now is the time for him to run, faster than storm-swift horses. In full armor Apollo son of Zeus leaps upon him, with the fire of the lightning. And in the murderer's track follow dreadful unfailing spirits of vengeance.

The word of Apollo has blazed out from snowy Parnassus[20] for all to see. Track down the unknown murderer by every means. He roams under cover of the wild forest, among caves and rocks, like a wild bull, wretched, cut off from mankind, his feet in pain. He turns his back on the prophecies delivered at the world's center, but they, alive forever, hover round him.

The wise prophet's words have brought me terror and confusion. I cannot agree with him, nor speak against him. I do not know what to say. I waver in hope and fear; I cannot see forward or back. What cause for quarrel was there between Oedipus and Laius? I never heard of one in time past; I know of none now.

I see no reason to attack the great fame of Oedipus in order to avenge the mysterious murder of Laius.

Zeus and Apollo, it is true, understand and know in full the events of man's life. But whether a mere man knows the truth—whether a human prophet knows more than I do—who is to be a fair judge of that? It is true that one man may be wiser than another. But I, for my part, will never join those who blame Oedipus, until I see these charges proved. We all saw how the Sphinx came against him—there his wisdom was proved. In that hour of danger he was the joy of Thebes. Remembering that day, my heart will never judge him guilty of evil action.

[Enter Creon, from side.]

CREON

Fellow citizens of Thebes, I am here in an angry mood. I hear that King Oedipus brings terrible charges against me. If, in the present dangerous situation, he thinks that I have injured him in any way, by word or deed, let me not live out the rest of my days with such a reputation. The damage done to me by such a report is no simple thing—it is the worst there is—to be called a traitor in the city, by all of you, by my friends.

CHORUS LEADER

This attack on you must have been forced out of him by anger; he lost control of himself.

CREON

Who told him that *I* advised Tiresias to make these false statements?

CHORUS LEADER

That's what was said—but I don't know what the intention was.

CREON

Were his eyes and mind unclouded when he made this charge against me?

CHORUS LEADER

I don't know. It is no use asking *me* about the actions of those who rule Thebes. Here is Oedipus. Look, he is coming out of the palace.

[Enter Oedipus, from door.]

OEDIPUS

[To Creon] You! What are you doing here? Do you have the face to come to my palace—you who are convicted as my murderer, exposed as a robber attempting to steal my throne? In God's name, tell me, what did you take me for when you made this plot—a coward? Or a fool? Did you think I wouldn't notice this conspiracy of yours creeping up on me in the dark? That once I saw it, I wouldn't defend myself? Don't you see that your plan is foolish—to hunt for a crown without numbers or friends behind you? A crown is won by numbers and money.

CREON

I have a suggestion. You in your turn listen to a reply as long as your speech, and, after you have heard me, *then* judge me.

OEDIPUS

You are a clever speaker, but I am a slow learner—from *you*. I have found you an enemy and a burden to me.

CREON

Just one thing, just listen to what I say.

OEDIPUS

Just one thing, don't try to tell me you are not a traitor.

CREON

Listen, if you think stubbornness deprived of intelligence is a worth-while possession, you are out of your mind.

OEDIPUS

Listen, if you think you can injure a close relative and then not pay for it, you are out of your mind.

CREON

All right, that's fair. But at least explain to me what I am supposed to have done.

OEDIPUS

Did you or did you not persuade me that I ought to send for that "holy" prophet?

CREON

Yes, I did, and I am still of the same mind.

OEDIPUS

Well then, how long is it since Laius . . . [*Pause.*]

CREON

Did what? I don't follow your drift.

OEDIPUS

Disappeared, vanished, violently murdered?

CREON

Many years ago; it is a long count back in time.

OEDIPUS

And at that time, was this prophet at his trade?

CREON
    Yes, wise as he is now, and honored then as now.

OEDIPUS
    Did he mention my name at that time?

CREON
    No, at least not in my presence.

OEDIPUS
    You investigated the murder of Laius, didn't you?

CREON
    We did what we could, of course. But we learned
nothing.

OEDIPUS
    How was it that this wise prophet did not say all this
then?

CREON
    I don't know. And when I don't understand, *I* keep
silent.

OEDIPUS
    Here's something you *do* know, and could say, too, if
you were a loyal man.

CREON
    What do you mean? If I know, I will not refuse to
answer.

OEDIPUS

Just this. If he had not come to an agreement with you, Tiresias would never have called the murder of Laius *my* work.

CREON

If that's what he says—you are the one to know. Now I claim my rights from you—answer my questions as I did yours just now.

OEDIPUS

Ask your questions. I shall not be proved a murderer.

CREON

You are married to my sister, are you not?

OEDIPUS

The answer to that question is yes.

CREON

And you rule Thebes jointly and equally with her?

OEDIPUS

She gets from me whatever she wants.

CREON

And I am on an equal basis with the two of you, isn't that right?

OEDIPUS

Yes, it is, and that fact shows what a disloyal friend you are.

CREON

    No, not if you look at it rationally, as I am explaining it to you. Consider this point first—do you think anyone would prefer to be supreme ruler and live in fear rather than to sleep soundly at night and still have the same power as the king? I am not the man to long for royalty rather than royal power, and anyone who has any sense agrees with me. As it is now, I have everything I want from you, and nothing to fear; but if I were king, I would have to do many things I have no mind to. How could the throne seem more desirable to me than power and authority which bring me no trouble? I can see clearly—all I want is what is pleasant and profitable at the same time. As it is now, I am greeted by all, everyone salutes me, all those who want something from you play up to me—that's the key to success for them. What makes you think I would give up all this and accept what you have? No, a mind which sees things clearly, as I do, would never turn traitor. I have never been tempted by such an idea, and I would never have put up with anyone who took such action.

    You can test the truth of what I say. Go to Delphi and ask for the text of the oracle, to see if I gave you an accurate report. One thing more. If you find that I conspired with the prophet Tiresias, then condemn me to death, not by a single vote, but by a double, yours and mine both. But do not accuse me in isolation, on private, baseless fancy. It is not justice to make the mistake of taking bad men for good, or good for bad. To reject a good friend is the equivalent of throwing away one's own dear life—that's my opinion. Given time you will realize all this without fail: time alone reveals the just man—the unjust you can recognize in one short day.

CHORUS LEADER

That is good advice, my lord, for anyone who wants to avoid mistakes. Quick decisions are not the safest.

OEDIPUS

When a plotter moves against me in speed and secrecy, then I too must be quick to counterplot. If I take my time and wait, then his cause is won, and mine lost.

CREON

What do you want then? Surely you don't mean to banish me from Thebes?

OEDIPUS

Not at all. Death is what I want for you, not exile.

CREON

You give a clear example of what it is to feel hate and envy.

OEDIPUS

You don't believe me, eh? You won't give way?

CREON

No, for I can see you don't know what you are doing.

OEDIPUS

Looking after my own interests.

CREON

And what about mine?

OEDIPUS

You are a born traitor.

CREON

And you don't understand anything.

OEDIPUS

Whether I do or not—I am in power here.

CREON

Not if you rule badly.

OEDIPUS

[To Chorus] Listen to him, Thebes, my city.

CREON

My city, too, not yours alone.

CHORUS LEADER

Stop, my lords. Here comes Jocasta from the house, in the nick of time. With her help, you must compose this quarrel between you.

[Enter Jocasta, from door.]

JOCASTA

Have you no sense, God help you, raising your voices in strife like this? Have you no sense of shame? The land is plague-stricken and you pursue private quarrels. *[To Oedipus]* You go into the house, and you, too,

Creon, inside. Don't make so much trouble over some small annoyance.

CREON

Sister, your husband, Oedipus, claims the right to inflict dreadful punishments on me. He will choose between banishing me from my fatherland and killing me.

OEDIPUS

Exactly. Jocasta, I caught him in a treacherous plot against my life.

CREON

May I never enjoy life, but perish under a curse, if I have done to you any of the things you charge me with.

JOCASTA

In God's name, Oedipus, believe what he says. Show respect for the oath he swore by the gods—do it for my sake and the sake of these people here.

CHORUS

Listen to her, King Oedipus. Think over your decision, take her advice, I beg you.

OEDIPUS

What concession do you want me to make?

CHORUS

Creon was no fool before, and now his oath increases his stature. Respect him.

OEDIPUS

Do you know what you are asking?

CHORUS

Yes, I know.

OEDIPUS

Tell me what it means, then.

CHORUS

This man is your friend—he has sworn an oath— don't throw him out dishonored on the strength of hearsay alone.

OEDIPUS

Understand this. If that is what you are after, you want me to be killed or banished from this land.

CHORUS

No. By the sun,[21] foremost of all the gods! May I perish miserably abandoned by man and God, if any such thought is in my mind. My heart is racked with pain for the dying land of Thebes—must you add new sorrows of your own making to those we already have?

OEDIPUS

Well then, let him go—even if it *does* lead to my death or inglorious banishment. It is *your* piteous speech that rouses my compassion—not what *he* says. As for him, I shall hate him, wherever he goes.

CREON

You show your sulky temper in giving way, just as you

did in your ferocious anger. Natures like yours are hardest to bear for their owners—and justly so.

OEDIPUS

Get out, will you? Out!

CREON

I am going. I found you ignorant—but these men think I am right.

[Exit Creon to side.]

CHORUS

[To Jocasta] Lady, why don't you get him into the house quickly?

JOCASTA

I will—when I have found out what happened here.

CHORUS

There was some ignorant talk based on hearsay and some hurt caused by injustice.

JOCASTA

On both sides?

CHORUS

Yes.

JOCASTA

And what did they say?

CHORUS

Enough, that is enough, it seems to me. I speak in the interests of the whole country. Let this matter lie where they left it.

OEDIPUS

You see where your good intentions have brought you. This is the result of turning aside and blunting the edge of my anger.

CHORUS

My king, I said it before, more than once—listen to me. I would be exposed as a madman, useless, brainless, if I were to turn my back on you. You found Thebes laboring in a sea of trouble, you righted her and set her on a fair course. All I wish now is that you should guide us as well as you did then.

JOCASTA

In God's name, explain to me, my lord—what was it made you so angry?

OEDIPUS

I will tell you. I have more respect for you than for these people here. Creon and his conspiracy against me, that's what made me angry.

JOCASTA

Tell me clearly, what was the quarrel between you?

OEDIPUS

He says that *I* am the murderer of Laius.

JOCASTA

On what evidence? His own knowledge, or hearsay?

OEDIPUS

Oh, he keeps his own lips clear of responsibility—he sent a swindling prophet in to speak for him.

JOCASTA

A prophet? In that case, rid your mind of your fear, and listen to me. I can teach you something. There is no human being born that is endowed with prophetic power. I can prove it to you—and in a few words.

A prophecy came to Laius once—I won't say from Apollo himself, but from his priests. It said that Laius was fated to die by the hand of his son, a son to be born to him and to me. Well, Laius, so the story goes, was killed by foreign robbers at a place where three highways meet. As for the son—three days after his birth Laius fastened his ankles together and had him cast away on the pathless mountains.

So, in this case, Apollo did not make the son kill his father or Laius die by his own son's hand, as he had feared. Yet these were the definite statements of the prophetic voices. Don't pay any attention to prophecies. If God seeks or needs anything, he will easily make it clear to us himself.

OEDIPUS

Jocasta, something I heard you say has disturbed me to the soul, unhinged my mind.

JOCASTA

What do you mean? What was it that alarmed you so?

OEDIPUS

I thought I heard you say that Laius was killed at a place where three highways meet.

JOCASTA

Yes, that's what the story was—and still is.

OEDIPUS

Where is the place where this thing happened?

JOCASTA

The country is called Phocis:[22] two roads, one from Delphi and one from Daulia, come together and form one.

OEDIPUS

When did it happen? How long ago?

JOCASTA

We heard the news here in Thebes just before you appeared and became King.

OEDIPUS

O God, what have you planned to do to me?

JOCASTA

What is it, Oedipus, which haunts your spirit so?

OEDIPUS

No questions, not yet. Laius—tell me what he looked like, how old he was.

JOCASTA

He was a big man—his hair had just begun to turn white. And he had more or less the same build as you.

OEDIPUS

O God! I think I have just called down on myself a dreadful curse—not knowing what I did.

JOCASTA

What do you mean? To look at you makes me shudder, my lord.

Tiresias   Thems

OEDIPUS

I am dreadfully afraid the blind prophet could see. But tell me one more thing that will throw light on this.

JOCASTA

I am afraid. But ask your question; I will answer if I can.

OEDIPUS

Was Laius poorly attended, or did he have a big bodyguard, like a king?

JOCASTA

There were five men in his party. One of them was a herald. And there was one wagon—Laius was riding in it.

OEDIPUS

Oh, it is all clear as daylight now. Who was it told you all this at the time?

JOCASTA

A slave from the royal household. He was the only one who came back.

OEDIPUS

Is he by any chance in the palace now?

JOCASTA

No, he is not. When he came back and saw you ruling in place of Laius, he seized my hand and begged me to send him to work in the country, to the pastures, to the flocks, as far away as I could—out of sight of Thebes. And I sent him. Though he was a slave he deserved this favor from me—and much more.

OEDIPUS

Can I get him back here, in haste?

JOCASTA

It can be done. But why are you so intent on this?

OEDIPUS

I am afraid, Jocasta, that I have said too much—that's why I want to see this man.

JOCASTA

Well, he shall come. But I have a right, it seems to me, to know what it is that torments you so.

OEDIPUS

So you shall. Since I am so full of dreadful expectation, I shall hold nothing back from you. Who else should I speak to, who means more to me than you, in this time of trouble?

My father was Polybus, a Dorian, and my mother Merope, of Corinth.[23] I was regarded as the greatest man in that city until something happened to me quite by chance, a strange thing, but not worth all the attention I paid it. A man at the banquet table, who had had too much to drink, told me, over his wine, that I was not the true son of my father. I was furious, but, hard though it was, I controlled my feelings, for that day at least. On the next day I went to my parents and questioned them. They were enraged against the man who had so taunted me. So I took comfort from their attitude, but still the thing tormented me—for the story spread far and wide. Without telling my parents, I set off on a journey to the oracle of Apollo, at Delphi. Apollo sent me away with my question unanswered but he foretold a dreadful, calamitous future for me—to lie with my mother and beget children men's eyes would not bear the sight of—and to be the killer of the father that gave me life.

When I heard that, I ran away. From that point on I measured the distance to the land of Corinth by the stars. I was running to a place where I would never see that shameful prophecy come true. On my way I came to the place in which you say this king, Laius, met his death.

I will tell you the truth, all of it. As I journeyed on I came near to this triple crossroad and there I was met by a herald and a man riding on a horse-drawn wagon, just as you described it. The driver, and the old man himself, tried to push me off the road. In anger I struck the driver as he tried to crowd me off. When the old man saw me coming past the wheels he aimed at my head with a two-pronged goad, and hit me. I paid him back in full, with interest: in no time at all he was hit by the stick I held in my hand and rolled backwards from the center of the wagon. I killed the whole lot of them.

Now, if this stranger had anything to do with Laius— is there a more unhappy man alive than I? Who could be more hateful to the gods than I am? No foreigner or citizen may take me into his house, no one can talk to me—everyone must expel me from his home. And the man who called down these curses on me was I myself, no one else. With these hands that killed him I defile the dead man's marriage bed. How can I deny that I am vile, utterly unclean? I must be banished from Thebes, and then I may not even see my own parents or set foot on my own fatherland—or else I am doomed to marry my own mother and kill my father Polybus, who brought me up and gave me life. I am the victim of some harsh divinity; what other explanation can there be?

Let it not happen, not that, I beg you, holy majesty of God, may I never see that day! May I disappear from among men without trace before I see such a stain of misfortune come upon me!

CHORUS LEADER
My lord, this makes us tremble. But do not despair—you have still to hear the story from the eye-witness.

OEDIPUS
That's right. That's my hope now, such as it is—to wait for the shepherd.

JOCASTA

Why all this urgency about his coming?

OEDIPUS

I'll tell you. If it turns out that he tells the same story as you—then I, at least, will be cleared of responsibility.

JOCASTA

What was so important in what you heard from me?

OEDIPUS

You said his story was that *several* robbers killed Laius. Well, if he speaks of the same number as you— then I am not the killer. For one could never be equal to many. But if he speaks of one man alone—then clearly the balance tips towards me as the killer.

JOCASTA

You can be sure that his account was made public just as I told it to you; he cannot go back on it, the whole city heard it, not I alone. But, my lord, even if he should depart from his former account in some particular, he still would never make the death of Laius what it was supposed to be—for Apollo said clearly that Laius was to be killed by my son. But that poor infant never killed Laius; it met its own death first. So much for prophecy. For all it can say, I would not, from now on, so much as look to right or left.

OEDIPUS

Yes, I agree. But all the same, that shepherd—send someone to fetch him. Do it at once.

JOCASTA

I shall send immediately. And now let us go in. I would not do anything except what pleases you.

[Exeunt Oedipus and Jocasta through doors.]

CHORUS

[Chanting in unison]

May Destiny be with me always;
Let me observe reverence and purity
In word and deed.
Laws that stand above have been established—
Born in the upper air on high;
Their only father is heaven;
No mortal nature, no man gave them birth.
They never forget, or sleep.
In them God is great, and He does not grow old.

The despot is the child of violent pride,
Pride that vainly stuffs itself
With food unseasonable, unfit,
Climbs to the highest rim
And then plunges sheer down into defeat
Where its feet are of no use.
Yet I pray to God to spare that vigor
Which benefits the state.
God is my protector, on Him I shall never cease
    to call.

The man who goes his way
Overbearing in word and deed,

Who fears no justice,
Honors no temples of the gods—
May an evil destiny seize him
And punish his ill-starred pride.
How shall such a man defend his life
Against God's arrows?
If such deeds as this are honored,
Why should we join the sacred dance and worship?

I shall go no more in reverence to Delphi,
The holy center of the earth,
Nor to any temple in the world,
Unless these prophecies come true,
For all men to point at in wonder.
O Zeus, King of heaven, ruler of all,
If you deserve this name,
Do not let your everlasting power be deceived,
Do not forget.
The old prophecies about Laius are failing,
Men reject them now.
Apollo is without honor everywhere.
The gods are defeated.

[Enter Jocasta, with branches of olive.]

JOCASTA
[To chorus] Lords of Thebes, it occurred to me to
come to the temples of the gods bearing in my hands
these branches and offerings of incense. For Oedipus is
distracted with sorrows of all kinds. He does not act like
a man in control of his reason, judging the present by
the past—he is at the mercy of anyone who speaks to
him, especially one who speaks of terrors. I have given

him advice, but it does no good. *[Facing the altar]* So I come to you, Lord Apollo, for you are closest to hand. I come in supplication with these emblems of prayer. Deliver us, make us free and clear of defilement. We are all afraid, like passengers on a ship who see their pilot crazed with fear.

[Enter from side Corinthian messenger.]

CORINTHIAN MESSENGER
[To chorus] Strangers, can one of you tell me— where is the palace of King Oedipus? Better still, if you know, where is the king himself?

CHORUS LEADER
This is his palace, and he is inside, stranger. This lady is his queen, his wife and mother of his children.

CORINTHIAN MESSENGER
Greetings to the noble wife of Oedipus! May you and all your family be blessed forever.

JOCASTA
The same blessings on you, stranger, for your kind words. But tell us what you want. Why have you come? Have you some news for us?

CORINTHIAN MESSENGER
Good news for your house and your husband, lady.

JOCASTA
What news? Who sent you?

CORINTHIAN MESSENGER

I come from Corinth. My message will bring you joy—no doubt of that—but sorrow, too.

JOCASTA

What is it? How can it work both ways?

CORINTHIAN MESSENGER

The people of Corinth will make Oedipus their king, so I heard there.

JOCASTA

What? Is old Polybus no longer on the throne?

CORINTHIAN MESSENGER

No. He is dead and in his grave.

JOCASTA

What did you say? Polybus is dead? Dead?

CORINTHIAN MESSENGER

Condemn me to death if I am not telling the truth.

JOCASTA

[To servant] You there, go in quickly and tell your master.

O prophecies of the gods, where are you now? Polybus was the man Oedipus feared he might kill— and so avoided him all this time. And now he's dead—a natural death, and not by the hand of Oedipus.

[Enter Oedipus, from doors.]

OEDIPUS
    Jocasta, why did you send for me to come out here?

JOCASTA
    Listen to what this man says, and see what has
become of the holy prophecies of the gods.

OEDIPUS
    Who is he? What does he have to say to me?

JOCASTA
    He's from Corinth. He came to tell you that your
father Polybus is dead and gone.

OEDIPUS
    Is this true? Tell me yourself.

CORINTHIAN MESSENGER
    If that's what you want to hear first, here it is, a plain
statement: Polybus is dead and gone.

OEDIPUS
    How? Killed by a traitor, or wasted by disease?

CORINTHIAN MESSENGER
    He was old. It did not take much to put him to sleep.

OEDIPUS
    By disease, then—that's how he died?

CORINTHIAN MESSENGER
    Yes, that, and the length of years he had lived.

OEDIPUS

So! Why then, Jocasta, should we study Apollo's oracle, or gaze at the birds screaming over our heads—those prophets who announced that I would kill my father? He's dead, buried, below ground. And here I am in Thebes—I did not put hand to sword.

Perhaps he died from longing to see me again. That way, it could be said that I was the cause of his death. But there he lies, dead, taking with him all these prophecies I feared—they are worth nothing!

JOCASTA

Is that not what I told you?

OEDIPUS

It is. But I was led astray by fear.

JOCASTA

Now rid your heart of fear forever.

OEDIPUS

No, I must still fear—and who would not?—a marriage with my mother.

JOCASTA

Fear? Why should man fear? His life is governed by the operations of chance. Nothing can be clearly foreseen. The best way to live is by hit and miss, as best you can. Don't be afraid that you may marry your mother. Many a man before you, in dreams, has shared his mother's bed. But to live at ease one must attach no importance to such things.

OEDIPUS

All that you have said would be fine—if my mother were not still alive. But she is, and no matter how good a case you make, I am still a prey to fear.

JOCASTA

But your father's death—that much at least is a great blessing.

OEDIPUS

Yes, I see that. But my mother, as long as she is alive, fills me with fear.

CORINTHIAN MESSENGER

Who is this woman that inspires such fear in you?

OEDIPUS

Merope, old man, the wife of Polybus.

CORINTHIAN MESSENGER

And what is there about her which frightens you?

OEDIPUS

A dreadful prophecy sent by the gods.

CORINTHIAN MESSENGER

Can you tell me what it is? Or is it forbidden for others to know?

OEDIPUS

Yes, I can tell you. Apollo once announced that I am destined to mate with my mother, and shed my father's blood with my own hand. That is why for so many years I have lived far away from Corinth. It has turned out well—but still, there's nothing sweeter than the sight of one's parents.

CORINTHIAN MESSENGER

Is that it? It was in fear of this that you banished yourself from Corinth?

OEDIPUS

Yes. I did not want to be my father's murderer.

CORINTHIAN MESSENGER

My lord, I do not know why I have not already released you from that fear. I came here to bring you good news.

OEDIPUS

If you can do that, you will be handsomely rewarded.

CORINTHIAN MESSENGER

Yes, that was why I came, to bring you home to Corinth, and be rewarded for it.

OEDIPUS

I will never go to the city where my parents live.

CORINTHIAN MESSENGER

My son, it is clear that you don't know what you are doing.

OEDIPUS

What do you mean, old man? In God's name, explain yourself.

CORINTHIAN MESSENGER

You don't know what you are doing, if you are afraid to come home because of *them*.

OEDIPUS

I am afraid that Apollo's prophecy may come true.

CORINTHIAN MESSENGER

That you will be stained with guilt through your parents?

OEDIPUS

Yes, that's it, old man, that's the fear which pursues me always.

CORINTHIAN MESSENGER

In reality, you have nothing to fear.

OEDIPUS

Nothing? How, if I am the son of Polybus and Merope?

CORINTHIAN MESSENGER

Because Polybus was not related to you in any way.

OEDIPUS

What do you mean? Was Polybus not my father?

CORINTHIAN MESSENGER

No more than I am—he was as much your father as I.

OEDIPUS

How can my father be on the same level as you who
are nothing to me?

CORINTHIAN MESSENGER

Because he was no more your father than I am.

OEDIPUS

Then why did he call me his son?

CORINTHIAN MESSENGER

He took you from my hands—I gave you to him.

OEDIPUS

Took me from your hands? Then how could he love
me so much?

CORINTHIAN MESSENGER

He had been childless, that was why he loved you.

OEDIPUS

You gave me to him? Did you . . . buy me? or find me
somewhere?

CORINTHIAN MESSENGER

I found you in the shady valleys of Mount Cithaeron.

OEDIPUS

What were you doing there?

CORINTHIAN MESSENGER

Watching over my flocks on the mountainside.

OEDIPUS
A shepherd, were you? A wandering day laborer?

CORINTHIAN MESSENGER
Yes, but at that moment I was your savior.

OEDIPUS
When you picked me up, was I in pain?

CORINTHIAN MESSENGER
Your ankles would bear witness on that point.

OEDIPUS
Oh, why do you speak of that old affliction?

CORINTHIAN MESSENGER
You had your ankles pinned together, and I freed you.

OEDIPUS
It is a dreadful mark of shame I have borne since childhood.

CORINTHIAN MESSENGER
From that misfortune comes the name which you still bear.°

OEDIPUS
In God's name, who did it? My mother, or my father? Speak.

° His name, Oedipus, means, in Greek, "swollen foot."

CORINTHIAN MESSENGER

I don't know. The one who gave you to me is the man to ask, not me.

OEDIPUS

You got me from someone else—you did not find me yourself?

CORINTHIAN MESSENGER

No. Another shepherd gave you to me.

OEDIPUS

Who was he? Do you know? Could you describe him?

CORINTHIAN MESSENGER

I think he belonged to the household of Laius.

OEDIPUS

You mean the man who was once king of this country?

CORINTHIAN MESSENGER

Yes. He was one of the shepherds of Laius.

OEDIPUS

Is he still alive? Can I talk to him?

CORINTHIAN MESSENGER

[To chorus] You people who live here would know that better than I.

OEDIPUS

[To chorus] Is there any one of you people here who knows this shepherd he mentioned? Has anyone seen him in the fields, or here in Thebes?

CHORUS LEADER

I think it is the same man from the fields you wanted to see before. But the queen here, Jocasta, could tell you that.

OEDIPUS

Jocasta, do you remember the man we sent for just now? Is *that* the man he is talking about?

JOCASTA

Why ask who he means? Don't pay any attention to him. Don't even think about what he said—it makes no sense.

OEDIPUS

What? With a clue like this? Give up the search? Fail to solve the mystery of my birth? Never!

JOCASTA

In God's name, if you place any value on your life, don't pursue the search. It is enough that *I* am sick to death.

OEDIPUS

You have nothing to be afraid of. Even if my mother turns out to be a slave, and I a slave for three generations back, *your* noble birth will not be called in question.

JOCASTA

Take my advice, I beg you—do not go on with it.

OEDIPUS

Nothing will move me. I *will* find out the whole truth.

JOCASTA

It is good advice I am giving you—I am thinking of you.

OEDIPUS

That "good advice" of yours is trying my patience.

JOCASTA

Ill-fated man. May you never find out who you are!

OEDIPUS

[To attendants] One of you go and get that shepherd, bring him here. We will leave *her* to pride herself on her royal birth.

JOCASTA

Unfortunate! That is the only name I can call you by now. I shall not call your name again—ever!

[Exit Jocasta to palace.]

[A long silence.]

CHORUS

Why has the queen gone, Oedipus, why has she rushed away in such wild grief? I am afraid that from this silence evil will burst out.

OEDIPUS

Burst out what will! I shall know my origin, mean though it be. Jocasta perhaps—she is proud, *like* a woman—feels shame at the low circumstances of my birth. But I count myself the son of Good Chance, the giver of success—I shall not be dishonored. Chance is my mother. My brothers are the months which have made me sometimes small and sometimes great. Such is my lineage and I shall not betray it. I will not give up the search for the truth about my birth.

[Exit Oedipus to palace.]

CHORUS

[Chanting in unison]

If I am a true prophet
And see clear in my mind,
Tomorrow at the full moon
Oedipus will honor Mount Cithaeron
As his nurse and mother.
Mount Cithaeron—our king's Theban birthplace!
We shall celebrate it in dance and song—
A place loved by our king.
Lord Apollo, may this find favor in your sight.

Who was it, Oedipus my son, who bore you?
Which of the nymphs that live so long
Was the bride of Pan[24] the mountain god?
Was your mother the bride of Apollo himself?

He loves the upland pastures.
Or was Hermes[25] your father?
Perhaps Dionysus who lives on the mountain peaks
Received you as a welcome gift
From one of the nymphs of Helicon,
His companions in sport.

*[Enter from side the shepherd, accompanied
by two guards.]*

[Enter Oedipus, from doors.]

OEDIPUS
    I never met the man, but, if I may make a guess, I think this man I see is the shepherd we have been looking for all this time. His age corresponds to that of the Corinthian here, and, in any case, the men bringing him are my servants, I recognize them.
    [To chorus leader] You have seen the shepherd before, you should know better than I.

CHORUS LEADER
    Yes, I recognize him. He was in the household of Laius—a devoted servant, and a shepherd.

OEDIPUS
    I question you first—you, the stranger from Corinth. Is this the man you spoke of?

CORINTHIAN MESSENGER
    This is the man.

OEDIPUS

[To shepherd] You, old man, come here. Look me in the face. Answer my questions. Were you a servant of Laius once?

SHEPHERD

I was. A slave. Not bought, though. I was born and reared in the palace.

OEDIPUS

What was your work? How did you earn your living?

SHEPHERD

For most of my life I have followed where the sheep flocks went.

OEDIPUS

And where did you graze your sheep most of the time?

SHEPHERD

Well, there was Mount Cithaeron, and all the country round it.

OEDIPUS

Do you know this man here? Did you ever see him before?

SHEPHERD

Which man do you mean? What would he be doing there?

OEDIPUS

This one, here. Did you ever come across him?

SHEPHERD

I can't say, right away. Give me time. I don't remember.

CORINTHIAN MESSENGER

No wonder he doesn't remember, master. He forgets, but I'll remind him, and make it clear. I am sure he knows very well how the two of us grazed our flocks on Cithaeron—he had two and I only one—we were together three whole summers, from spring until the rising of Arcturus in the fall. When winter came I used to herd my sheep back to their winter huts, and he took his back to the farms belonging to Laius. Do you remember any of this? Isn't that what happened?

SHEPHERD

What you say is true, but it was a long time ago.

CORINTHIAN MESSENGER

Well, then, tell me this. Do you remember giving me a child, a boy, for me to bring up as my own?

SHEPARD

What are you talking about? Why do you ask that question?

CORINTHIAN MESSENGER

Oedipus here, my good man, Oedipus and that child are one and the same.

SHEPHERD

Damn you! Shut your mouth. Keep quiet!

OEDIPUS

Old man, don't you correct *him*. It is you and your tongue that need correction.

SHEPHERD

What have I done wrong, noble master?

OEDIPUS

You refuse to answer his question about the child.

SHEPHERD

That's because he does not know what he's talking about—he is just wasting your time.

OEDIPUS

If you won't speak willingly, we shall see if pain can make you speak.

[The guards seize the shepherd.]

SHEPHERD

In God's name, don't! Don't torture me. I am an old man.

OEDIPUS

One of you twist his arms behind his back, quickly!

SHEPHERD

Oh, God, what for? What more do you want to know?

OEDIPUS

Did you give him the child he asked about?

SHEPHERD

Yes, I did. And I wish I had died that day.

OEDIPUS

You will die now, if you don't give an honest answer.

SHEPHERD

And if I speak, I shall be even worse off.

OEDIPUS

[To guards] What? More delay?

SHEPHERD

No! No! I said it before—I gave him the child.

OEDIPUS

Where did *you* get it? Was it yours? Or did it belong to someone else?

SHEPHERD

It wasn't mine. Someone gave it to me.

OEDIPUS

Which of these Thebans here? From whose house did it come?

SHEPHERD

In God's name, master, don't ask any more questions.

OEDIPUS
    You are a dead man if I have to ask you again.

SHEPHERD
    It was a child born in the house of Laius.

OEDIPUS
    Was it a slave? Or a member of the royal family?

SHEPHERD
    Oh, God, here comes the dreadful truth. And I must
speak.

OEDIPUS
    And I must hear it. But hear it I will.

SHEPHERD
    It was the son of Laius, so I was told. But the lady
inside there, your wife, she is the one to tell you.

OEDIPUS
    Did *she* give it to you?

SHEPARD
    Yes, my lord, she did.

OEDIPUS
    For what purpose?

SHEPHERD
    To destroy it.

OEDIPUS
Her own child?

SHEPHERD
She was afraid of dreadful prophecies.

OEDIPUS
What were they?

SHEPHERD
The child would kill its parents, that was the story.

OEDIPUS
Then why did you give it to this old man here?

SHEPHERD
In pity, master. I thought he would take it away to a foreign country—to the place he came from. If you are the man he says you are, you were born the most unfortunate of men.

OEDIPUS
O God! It has all come true. Light, let this be the last time I see you. I stand revealed—born in shame, married in shame, an unnatural murderer.

[Exit Oedipus into palace.]

[Exeunt others at sides.]

CHORUS

O generations of mortal men,
I add up the total of your lives
And find it equal to nothing.
What man wins more happiness
Than a mere appearance which quickly fades away?
With your example before me,
Your life, your destiny, miserable Oedipus,
     I call no man happy.

Oedipus outranged all others
And won complete prosperity and happiness.
He destroyed the Sphinx, that maiden
With curved claws and riddling songs,
And rose up like a towered wall against death—
Oedipus, savior of our city.
From that time on you were called King,
You were honored above all men,
Ruling over great Thebes.

And now—is there a man whose story is more
     pitiful?
His life is lived in merciless calamity and pain—
A complete reversal from his happy state.
O Oedipus, famous king,
You whom the same great harbor sheltered
As child and father both,
How could the furrows which your father plowed
Bear *you* in silence for so long?

Time, which sees all things, has found you out;
It sits in judgment on the unnatural marriage

Which was both begetter and begot.
    O son of Laius,
I wish I had never seen you.
I weep, like a man wailing for the dead.
    This is the truth:
You returned me to life once
And now you have closed my eyes in darkness.

[Enter, from the palace, a messenger.]

MESSENGER

Citizens of Thebes, you who are most honored in this city! What dreadful things you will see and hear! What a cry of sorrow you will raise, if, as true Thebans, you have any feeling for the royal house. Not even the great rivers of Ister and Phasis[26] could wash this house clean of the horrors it hides within. And it will soon expose them to the light of day—horrors deliberately willed, not involuntary. Those calamities we inflict on ourselves are those which cause the most pain.

CHORUS LEADER

The horrors we knew about before were burden enough. What other dreadful news do you bring?

MESSENGER

Here is the thing quickest for me to say and you to hear. Jocasta, our queen, is dead.

CHORUS LEADER

Poor lady. From what cause?

MESSENGER

By her own hand. You are spared the worst of what
has happened—you were not there to see it. But as far
as my memory serves, you shall hear the full story of
that unhappy woman's sufferings.

She came in through the door in a fury of passion
and rushed straight towards her marriage bed, tearing
at her hair with both hands. Into her bedroom she
went, and slammed the doors behind her. She was calling the name of Laius, so long dead, remembering the
child she bore to him so long ago—the child by whose
hand Laius was to die, and leave her, its mother, to bear
monstrous children to her own son. She wailed in
mourning for her marriage, in which she had borne
double offspring, a husband from her husband and children from her child. And after that—but I do not know
exactly how she died. For Oedipus came bursting in,
shouting, and so we could not watch Jocasta's suffering
to the end; all of us looked at him as he ran to and fro.
He rushed from one of us to the other, asking us to give
him a sword, to tell him where he could find his wife—
no, not his wife, but his mother, his mother and the
mother of his children.

It must have been some supernatural being that
showed the raving man where she was; it was not one of
us. As if led by a guide he threw himself against the
doors of her room with a terrible cry; he bent the bolts
out of their sockets, and so forced his way into the
room. And there we saw Jocasta, hanging, her neck
caught in a swinging noose of rope. When Oedipus saw
her he gave a deep dreadful cry of sorrow and loosened
the rope round her neck. And when the poor woman
was lying on the ground—then we saw the most dread-

ful sight of all. He ripped out the golden pins with which her clothes were fastened, raised them high above his head, and speared the pupils of his eyes. "You will not see," he said, "the horrors I have suffered and done. Be dark forever now—eyes that saw those you should never have seen, and failed to recognize those you longed to see." Murmuring words like these he raised his hands and struck his eyes again, and again. And each time the wounded eyes sent a stream of blood down his chin, no oozing flow but a dark shower of it, thick as a hailstorm.

These are the sorrows which have burst out and overwhelmed them both, man and wife alike. The wealth and happiness they once had was real while it lasted, but now—weeping, destruction, death, shame—name any shape of evil you will, they have them all.

CHORUS

And Oedipus—poor wretched Oedipus—has he now some rest from pain?

MESSENGER

He is shouting, "Open the doors, someone: show me to all the people of Thebes, my father's killer, my mother's"—I cannot repeat his unholy words. He speaks of banishing himself from Thebes, says he will not remain in his house under the curse which he himself pronounced. But he has no strength: he needs someone to guide his steps. The pain is more than he can bear.

But he will show you himself. The bolts of this door are opening. Now you will see a spectacle that even his enemies would pity.

[Enter Oedipus from door, blind.]

CHORUS

O suffering dreadful for mankind to see, most dreadful of all I ever saw. What madness came over you? What unearthly spirit, leaping farther than the mind can conceive, swooped down on your destiny? I pity you. I have many questions to ask you, much I wish to know; my eyes are drawn towards you—but I cannot bear to look. You fill me with horror.

OEDIPUS

Where am I going? Pity me! Where does my voice range to through the air? O spirit, what a leap you made!

CHORUS

To a point of dread, too far for men's ears and eyes.

OEDIPUS

Darkness, dark cloud all around me, enclosing me, unspeakable darkness, irresistible—you came to me on a wind that seemed favorable. Ah, I feel the stab of these sharp pains, and with it the memory of my sorrow.

CHORUS

In such torment it is no wonder that your pain and mourning should be double.

OEDIPUS

My friend! You are by my side still, you alone. You still stay by me, looking after the blind man. I know you are there. I am in the dark, but I can distinguish your voice clearly.

CHORUS

You have done a dreadful thing. How could you bring yourself to put out the light of your eyes? What superhuman power urged you on?

OEDIPUS

It was Apollo, friends, Apollo, who brought to fulfillment all my sufferings. But the hand that struck my eyes was mine and mine alone. What use had I for eyes? Nothing I could see would bring me joy.

CHORUS

It was just as you say.

OEDIPUS

What was there for me to look at, to speak to, to love? What joyful word can I expect to hear, my friends? Take me away, out of this country, quickly, take me away. I am lost, accursed, and hated by the gods beyond all other men.

CHORUS

I am moved to pity by your misfortunes and your understanding of them, too. I wish I had never known you!

OEDIPUS

A curse on the man who freed my feet from the cruel bonds on the mountain, who saved me and rescued me from death. He will get no thanks from me. I might have died then and there; but now I am a source of grief for myself and all who love me.

CHORUS

I wish it had turned out that way, too.

OEDIPUS

I would never have become my father's killer, never have been known to all men as my own mother's husband. Now I am godforsaken, the son of an accursed marriage, my own father's successor in the marriage bed. If there is any evil worse than the worst that a man can suffer—Oedipus has drawn it for his lot.

CHORUS

I cannot say you made the right decision. You would have been better dead than blind.

OEDIPUS

What I have done was the best thing to do. Don't read me any more lessons, don't give me any more advice. With what eyes could I have faced my father in the house of the dead, or my poor mother? I have done things to them both for which hanging is too small a punishment.

Do you think I longed to look at my children, born the way they were? No, not with these eyes of mine, never! Not this town either, its walls, its holy temples of the gods. From all of this I am cut off, I, the most nobly raised in Thebes, cut off by my own act. It was I who proclaimed that everyone should expel the impious man—the man the gods have now revealed as unholy—and the son of Laius. After I had exposed my own guilt—and what a guilt!—do you think I could have looked at my fellow citizens with steady eyes?

No, no! If there had been some way to block the

source of hearing, I would not have held back: I would have isolated my wretched body completely, so as to see and hear nothing at all. If my mind could be put beyond reach of my miseries—that would be my pleasure.

O Cithaeron, why did you receive me? Why did you not take and kill me on the spot, so that I should never reveal my origin to mankind?

O Polybus, and Corinth, and the ancient house I thought was my father's—what a handsome heir you raised up in me, how rotten beneath the surface! For now I am exposed—evil and born in evil.

O three roads in the deep valley, you oak wood and you narrow pass where the three roads meet, you who soaked up my father's blood, spilled by my hand—do you remember me? Do you remember what I did there, and what I did when I came here?

O marriage, marriage! You gave me birth, and then bred up seed from the one you brought into the world. You made an incestuous breed of father, brother, son— bride, wife, mother—all the most shameful things known to man.

But I must not speak of things that should never have been done. Quickly, in God's name, hide me somewhere outside Thebes, kill me, throw me into the sea, where you will never see me again.

Come close to me. I am a man of sorrow, but take courage and touch me. Do not be afraid; do what I ask. The evil is mine; no one but me can bear its weight.

[Enter Creon, from side, with attendants.]

CHORUS LEADER
Here is Creon. He will listen to your request.

Decision and action are up to him, now that he has taken your place as the sole ruler of Thebes.

OEDIPUS

What shall I say to him? What justification, what grounds for trust can I present? In everything I did to him before, I have been proved wrong.

CREON

I have not come to mock you, Oedipus, nor to reproach you for the wrong you did.

[*To attendants*] If you have no respect for the feelings of human beings, at least show reverence for the sunlight which nourishes all men. Do not leave him there in full view, an object of dread and horror which appalls the holy rain and the daylight. Get him into the palace as fast as you can.

[*The attendants move over to Oedipus, and stand by him until the end of the scene.*]

Only his family should see the family shame; this public spectacle is indecent.

OEDIPUS

In God's name—since you have exceeded my hopes and come in so generous a spirit to one so low—do something for me. I ask it in your interest, not mine.

CREON

What is it you are so anxious to have me do?

OEDIPUS

Banish me from this country as fast as you can—to a place where no man can see me or speak to me.

CREON

You can be sure I would have done so already, but first I wanted to ask the god Apollo what should be done.

OEDIPUS

But his command was clear, every word of it; death for the unholy man, the father-killer.

CREON

That *is* what the oracle said. But all the same, in our situation, it is better to inquire what should be done.

OEDIPUS

Will you consult Apollo about anyone as miserable as I?

CREON

Yes, and this time, I take it, you will believe what the god says.

OEDIPUS

Yes. I command you—and beg you—the woman in the palace, see to her burial. She is your sister, you are the man to do this. As for me, do not condemn this city of my fathers to shelter me within its walls, but let me live on the mountain, on Cithaeron, forever linked with my name, the mountain which my mother and father while they still lived chose as my burial place. Let me die there where they tried to kill me.

And yet I know this—no disease or anything else will destroy me. Otherwise I would never have been saved from death in the first place. I was saved—for some strange and dreadful end.

Well, let my destiny go where it will. As for my children, do not concern yourself about the boys, Creon. They are men; and will always find a way to live, wherever they may be. But my two poor helpless girls,[27] who were always at my table, who shared the same food I ate—take care of them for me.

What I wish for most is this. Let me touch them with these hands, as I weep for my sorrows. Please, my lord! Grant my prayer, generous man! If I could hold them I would think I had them with me, as I did when I could see.

*[Antigone and Ismene are led in from
the door by a nurse.]*

What's that? I hear something. Oh, God. It is my daughters, weeping. Creon took pity on me, and sent them to me, my dearest ones, my children. Am I right?

CREON

Yes, you are. I did this for you knowing the joy you always took in them, the joy you feel now.

OEDIPUS

Bless you for it! May you be rewarded for sending them. May God watch over you better than He did over me.

Children, where are you? Come here, come to these hands of mine, your brother's hands, the hands that intervened to make your father's once bright eyes so dim. Blind and thoughtless, I became your father, and your mother was my mother, too. I weep for you—see you I cannot—when I think of your future, the bitter life you will lead, the way men will treat you. What gatherings will you go to, what festivals, without returning home in tears, instead of taking part in the ceremonies?

And when you come to the age of marriage, who will take the risk, my daughters, and shoulder the burden of reproach which will be directed at my children—and yours? No reproach is missing. Your father killed his father. He sowed the field from which he himself had sprung, and begot you, his children, at the source of his own being. These are the reproaches you will hear. And who will marry you? There is no one who will do so, children; your destiny is clear—to waste away unmarried, childless.

Creon, you are the only father they have now, for we who brought them into the world are both of us destroyed. Do not abandon them to wander husbandless in poverty: they are your own flesh and blood. Do not make them equal to me and my miserable state, but pity them. They are children, they have no protector but you. Promise me this, noble Creon, touch me with your hand to confirm your promise.

And you, children—if you were old enough to understand, I would have much advice to give you. But as it is, I will tell you what to pray for. Pray that you may find a place where you are allowed to live, and for a life happier than your father's.

CREON

You have wept long enough. Now go inside the house.

OEDIPUS

I must obey, though it gives me no pleasure.

CREON

Yes, everything is good in its proper place and time.

OEDIPUS

I will go in then, but on one condition.

CREON

Tell me what it is. I am listening.

OEDIPUS

You must send me into exile—away from Thebes.

CREON

What you ask for is a gift only Apollo can grant.

OEDIPUS

But I am hateful to the gods above all men.

CREON

In that case, they will grant your request at once.

OEDIPUS

You consent, then?

CREON

It is not my habit to say what I don't mean.

OEDIPUS

Then take me away from here at once.

CREON

Come then, but let go of the children.

OEDIPUS

No, don't take them away from me.

CREON

Don't try to be master in everything. What you once won and held did not stay with you all your life long.

The following speech, for reasons too technical to discuss here, is considered by many authorities to be an addition to the play made by a later producer. The translator shares this opinion, but the lines are printed here for those who wish to use them.

CHORUS

Citizens who dwell in Thebes, look at Oedipus here, who knew the answer to the famous riddle and was a power in the land. On his good fortune all the citizens gazed with envy. Into what a stormy sea of dreadful trouble he has come now. Therefore we must call no man happy while he waits to see his last day, not until he has passed the border of life and death without suffering pain.

NOTES

---

1. **Oedipus:** King of Thebes, son of Laius and Jocasta. His name means "swollen footed."
2. **Thebes:** City in central Greece, site of one of the main legendary cycles of Greek mythology, the cycle of the House of Cadmus. Laius, father of Oedipus, was one of the most important kings of the house of Thebes.
3. **Zeus:** The father of the Olympian gods and the supreme ruler of the pantheon of Greek gods.
4. **two temples of Athena:** Athena, offspring of Zeus (she emerged fully grown directly from his forehead), was revered as patron goddess by the inhabitants of many cities in central Greece.
5. **Apollo/Ismenus:** According to the Greek epic poet Hesiod, Apollo was the son of Zeus and Leto, and brother of the goddess Artemis. One of the many shrines in Apollo's honor was by the river Ismenus, which flowed near Thebes.
6. **black god of death:** Hades, the brother of Zeus,

and ruler of the underworld, where the dead go on living but only as miserable shadows.

7. **Sphinx:** Egyptian symbolic creature with a lion's body and the head of a woman. Famed among the Greeks as a concealer of mysteries. The Sphinx had been besetting travelers outside Thebes with a riddling question: "What walks on four feet in the morning, two feet at noon, and three feet at night?" If the person could not answer correctly, the Sphinx killed and ate the traveler. Only Oedipus was able to answer this riddle: "man," because he crawls as a baby, walks as an adult, and walks with a cane as an old man.

8. **Creon:** Brother of Jocasta.

9. **oracle of Apollo:** As a god associated with light, intelligence, and justice, Apollo was frequently consulted as an oracle. His Pythian shrine, on the slopes of Mt. Parnassus, was thought to be holy and reliable.

10. **Lord of Delos:** Apollo was believed to have been born on the isolated island of Delos, in the Aegean Sea.

11. **Artemis:** The daughter of Zeus and Leto, and brother of Apollo. Her shrines were often located in the marketplace *(agora)* of the cities where worship of her was active.

12. **far-shooting Apollo:** A stock epithet for the god.

13. **War-god:** Ares was the son of Zeus and Hera. He was considered the god of plagues and pestilence, as well as of war itself.

14. **Thracian coasts:** Thrace was a favorite hangout of Ares. It is located in northeastern Greece, east of present-day Macedonia.

15. **Dionysus:** Dionysus was the son of Zeus and Semele—who was the daughter of Cadmus and was thus intimately involved with the House of Thebes. Dionysus was associated with fertility and the abundance of nature and was often accompanied by wildly dancing and celebrating women, who would have been a rarity in patriarchal Athens.

16. **Agenor:** Legendary king of Phoenicia, and father of Cadmus, who was the source of the Theban line.

17. **Tiresias:** A famous prophet of Thebes, blinded by Athena after he had seen her naked. In compensation he was later given the gift of prophecy. He exercised that gift in Thebes, as interpreter of the strange plague gripping the city.

18. **Mount Cithaeron:** Mountain southwest of Thebes on the border between Attica and Boeotia.

19. **Delphi:** Oracular shrine in central Greece, from which Apollo or his priests/priestesses often uttered mysterious and influential prophecies.

20. **Parnassus:** Mountain in central Greece. Delphi was situated at its foot.

21. **by the sun:** Helios, god of the sun, can see and observe all things and is thus a perfect witness to human affairs.

22. **Phocis:** A region in central Greece; Delphi was located there. Daulia was to the south of Mt. Parnassus.

23. **Corinth:** A city on the northern coast of the Peloponnese; the home of Polybus and Merope, the foster parents of Oedipus. *Dorian* refers to the settlers of the northern Peloponnese and the Isthmus of Corinth.

24. **Pan:** A woodland god, part man, part goat.

25. **Hermes:** Son of Zeus and Maia; messenger god, trickster, as well as deity of fields and woodlands.

26. **Ister and Phasis:** The Greeks believed that the Ister (part of the Danube) was the largest river in Europe. The Phasis is a big river whose source is in the Caucasus; it flows into the Black Sea.

27. **helpless girls:** Antigone and Ismene. Antigone will accompany Oedipus on his tragic journey away from Thebes, toward Colonus.

INTERPRETIVE NOTES

Plot

A boastful, confident Oedipus first appears as the savior of the suffering Theban people and promises to relieve their afflictions by tracking down the murderer of Laius. The chorus laments the situation in Thebes and begs the gods for mercy. Oedipus calls down a curse on the murderer of Laius.

At the suggestion of Creon, his brother-in-law, Oedipus sends for the seer Tiresias. The prophet at first refuses to speak, then finally accuses Oedipus himself of the murder. The chorus expresses its belief that the unknown murderer is doomed, but refuses to accept Tiresias' accusation of Oedipus. Oedipus accuses Creon of commanding the prophet to make a fake accusation, and the two of them quarrel. Jocasta ends their argument by explaining that Laius' baby son had been exposed on the hills and left to die and that Laius was killed by several robbers at the intersection of three roads.

Oedipus is not reassured—he remembers his own past encounter at a three-road intersection—and questions Jocasta in detail about the murder. In the face of mounting evidence, Oedipus holds to the fact that the sole surviving witness saw that Laius was murdered by more than one person. Oedipus calls in the witness. The chorus of Theban elders fears the worst.

A messenger from Corinth announces that Oedipus' "father," Polybus, is dead. Jocasta and Oedipus rejoice because they feel this disproves the prophecy that he will murder his father, but Oedipus still fears the prediction that he will marry his mother. The messenger then reveals that he had been asked to expose Oedipus by another herdsman, and that Oedipus has been raised by foster parents. Jocasta cries with terror, imploring Oedipus not to pursue the inquiry any further, but Oedipus, declaring he is not afraid of lowly birth, determines to continue. The chorus exults in the belief that Oedipus is a god-born foundling of the land of Thebes.

The Theban herdsman is led in and is at once identified by the messenger from Corinth as the one who gave him the baby to expose. Gradually the Theban herdsman is made to reveal that the baby was given to him by Jocasta. Oedipus now knows all and storms out. The chorus laments the inevitable tragedy of their great king.

A messenger from the house reports that Jocasta has hanged herself and Oedipus has put out his eyes. Oedipus is led in, begging the chorus to either banish or kill him. Creon takes Oedipus into the palace, where the ruined king begs for a final meeting with his two daughters, Antigone and Ismene. Oedipus wishes to be sent out into the wilderness, but must wait for Apollo's judgment. The chorus concludes with the thought "Consider no man happy while he waits to see his last day."

Characters

Oedipus. King, hero, and savior of Thebes and husband of Queen Jocasta. He is proud, hot-tempered, forceful, ready to find the truth, and genuinely concerned for his people and state. He fully satisfies Aristotle's dictum, in the *Poetics,* that the best tragic hero will be "a man who is not eminently good and just, yet whose misfortune is brought about not by vice or depravity, but by some error or frailty." This kind of hero, which Oedipus is, evokes from us those cleansing virtues of pity and fear, which make the tragic experience (its *catharsis*) ennobling for us.

Jocasta. Queen of Thebes, wife and—we learn—mother of Oedipus. She grows increasingly anxious as the play advances.

Creon. Brother of Jocasta, brother-in-law of Oedipus. He is cautious and bureaucratic, a rule giver and follower, a man who knows that the gods and fate can be terrible, and that it is better to keep your head down. Like Jocasta, and like the remorseless prophet Tiresias, Creon is a relatively one-dimensional figure, but perfect for the role assigned him, that of the conscientious maintainer of the status quo. His ideology is close to that of the Theban elders who make up the chorus.

Tiresias. A powerful blind prophet.

The Elders of Thebes. The chorus, who express the feelings of the populace.

Antigone and Ismene. Daughters of Oedipus and Jocasta.

Themes and Symbols

Fate vs. Free Will. The nature of fate and free will is complex and sometimes mysterious in *Oedipus*. On the one hand, we know that it is Apollo, an infallible god, who predicts that Oedipus will carry out the tragic sequence of events that unfolds in the play. Believing this, there is no way to see how Oedipus, as we meet him standing before the citizens of Thebes, can escape his doom. On the other hand, Oedipus charges boldly into the fatal drama facing him, looking under every stone to find the truth, though everyone else in the play urges him to hold back. He behaves in every way like a free man, making a series of choices, and disregarding the advice and warnings that surround him. We are left to wonder whether a humbler man, less inclined to boldness, with a more modest, less heroic history—say, a man like Creon—would have been able to avoid Oedipus' end. In fact, the chorus worries throughout the play that Oedipus' boldness and Jocasta's skepticism will somehow bring down a tragic fate upon the characters. The polarity of freedom and fate is never fully resolved in the play. Instead, the tension between the two of them feeds the relentless energy that seems to fuel Oedipus' journey toward his tragic fate. Many poets, theologians, and philosophers since Sophocles have puzzled over the roles that fate and free will play in human lives, but the unfolding of *Oedipus* gives us one of the most perfect examples of these intertwining elements of our experience.

Persistence of Truth and the Recognition of Truth. As both a philosopher and a dramatist, Sophocles makes much of the way the truth seems to persist in making itself known in spite of all efforts to conceal it, ignore it, or simply allow the past to swallow it up. In *Oedipus,* the forces of chance are entirely on the side of truth, and Oedipus finally accepts that truth, even though it is both improbable and impossibly hard to bear. In Aristotle's *Poetics,* this kind of recognition *(anagnorisis)* was a trademark of the tragic experience, and Sophocles ensures that the audience will feel it by having Oedipus recognize many smaller truths before facing the final, inevitable conclusion to which they lead him. It is not until the servant/herdsman from Thebes proclaims the last truth—that the child had been exposed by order of Jocasta, to avert the oracle—that the truth absolutely forces itself on Oedipus. He cries out, in the most dreadful of recognition scenes, "O God! It has all come true. Light, let this be the last time I see you. I stand revealed—born in shame, married in shame, an unnatural murderer." By the final scene of the play he is like the prophet Tiresias—literally blinded by the truth.

High Tragic Knowledge vs. the Wisdom of the People. Oedipus' recognition of the truth, terrible as it is, is but the first step in a series that will qualify him as having reached the highest possible level of understanding of the human condition, an understanding only available to the greatest of tragic heroes. When he reaches this understanding in Sophocles' last play, *Oedipus at Colonus*, Oedipus is "taken up" into the realm of the "gods," of ultimate understanding.

A far different kind of knowledge and understanding is allocated to the chorus in Sophocles' tragedies. The Theban elders who make up the chorus in *Oedipus* fear the worst, vacillate between ill-founded exhilaration and precautionary despair, and on the whole counsel only moderation and prudence, in dealing with the dark secrets of the past. These experienced elders know that the truth is likely to turn out bitter, but cannot at the moment penetrate the truth that Tiresias knows by blinding intuition.

Seeing, Sight, Insight, and Blindness. As the above comments make clear, the primary metaphors for truth, lies, and truth-seeking in *Oedipus* all revolve around vision. Oedipus cannot see the truth of his life as it stands before him. On the other hand, he has seen far too much, as has Jocasta. The truth appears to be buried out of sight and then comes out into the open through the words of a blind prophet and a herdsman (whose job, after all, is to oversee the animals). And of course Oedipus' final, dramatic offstage act is to blind himself. It is also clear that the link between truth and sight remains strong today—we are still accustomed to speaking of truth in terms of blindness and insight.

Other readers, such as Sigmund Freud, the father of psychoanalysis (see below) have gone beyond these clear metaphors to see the blindness and sight in *Oedipus* as symbolic of other psychic states.

Tragic Action and Sexuality. Sigmund Freud drew international attention to the relationship between tragedy and sexuality in his *Introductory Lectures on Psychoanalysis* (1916–17), and *Oedipus* was his greatest, most notorious example of his theories. Freud argued that around the age of three or four, male children develop a jealous desire to kill their fathers and marry their mothers. He saw in Oedipus' slaying of Laius and marriage to Jocasta a playing out of this theoretical complex, dubbed the Oedipus complex. Though the universality of Freud's theories has since been challenged, their vitality points to Sophocles' profound grasp of the human problems of desire, jealousy, ambition, and self-deception, and the intractable nature of human sexuality. For Freud, sexuality was like the great truths that Oedipus both seeks and flees: unspeakable, hidden, but also unavoidable and exposed in plain sight if only we had eyes to see it.

CRITICAL EXCERPTS

Note: The play *Oedipus the King* is also known as *Oedipus Tyrannus* and *Oedipus Rex*.

Historical/Cultural/Philosophical Background

Friedrich Nietzsche. "The Birth of Tragedy" (1871). Trans. Michael Lebeck. In Thomas Woodard, *Sophocles: A Collection of Critical Essays*. Englewood Cliffs, NJ: Prentice-Hall, 1966.

A searching text by the great German philosopher and classicist. He plumbs the blend of serenity and horror that marked Greek tragedy, not to mention the greatest works of Greek art and architecture.

The most pathetic figure of the Greek theater, the unfortunate Oedipus, Sophocles takes to be a noble man, called to error and alienation in spite of his wisdom, yet called too, in the end, through monstrous suffering, to radiate a magic power rich in a blessing, which works even after he passes on. "The noble man does not sin" is what the poet means. Though every natural law, the whole civilized world, fall to the ground through his actions, these very actions attract a higher, magical circle of influences which grounds a new world upon the rubble of the old.

H. D. F. Kitto. *Greek Tragedy*. London: Methuen and Co., 1939.

Still the most readable introduction to the whole literary culture of ancient Greek tragedy.

When therefore we say that the Greek dramatist was an artist, we are not using a tired platitude meaning that he preferred pretty verses and plots to ill-made ones; we mean that he felt, thought, and worked like a painter or a musician, not like a philosopher or a teacher. Being a dramatist, he must deal with moral or intellectual questions, and what he says about them is a natural subject of study; but if we are to treat the plays as plays and not as documents we must, as in criticizing painting, free ourselves from the "tyranny of the subject." If we can grope our way to the fundamental tragic conception of each play or group of plays, we can hope to explain their form and style.

John Jones. *On Aristotle and Greek Tragedy*. New York: Oxford University Press, 1962.

Jones uses Aristotle's influential *Poetics* (350 BC) to explore texts of Greek tragedy, and at the same time to bring out many fresh aspects of the three great Athenian tragedians.

This work, which we always call the *Poetics*, has no rival among commentaries on the tragic drama of the Greeks. Its finish is rough, sometimes suggesting lecture notes rather than literary composition; and its second book has disappeared in which Aristotle dealt with comedy and other subjects. But it is the only extended critical and theoretical record to survive from the civilization that produced the plays. And that would be decisive, even if its intrinsic merit were less than it is.

Albin Lesky. *Greek Tragedy*. Trans. Frankfort. New York: Barnes and Noble, 1979.

A survey of the whole achievement of Greek tragedy, this book casts new light on ancient texts by juxtaposing them with modern texts and critical opinions.

Any attempt to define tragedy should begin with the words spoken by Goethe on the 6th of June, 1824, to Chancellor Mueller: "All tragedy depends on an insoluble conflict. As soon as harmony is obtained or becomes a possibility tragedy vanishes." Here the problem we are trying to solve has been grasped at the root. And yet these words contribute to its solution no more than a fairly wide frame of reference, because the statement that tragedy implies insoluble conflict says nothing about the nature of the opposing forces. It will be an imperative task to define this "conflict" with more precision in every sphere of tragedy, in art as in real life. This proves particularly fruitful in Greek tragedy, where the types of conflict . . . reside within the realm of the gods, or denote a polar tension between god and man; or again . . . may be a matter of conflicting elements within a man's breast.

Simon Goldhill. *Reading Greek Tragedy*. Cambridge: Cambridge University Press, 1986.

A wide-ranging study of Greek tragedy—and other classical Greek texts—from the perspective of their concern with language.

The continuing response to Greek tragedy is not simply each generation, each reader or each reader at different times, reaching towards some eternally fixed beauty or immutable truth encapsulated in the glory that was Greek tragedy, but being faced with the problems, tensions and uncertainties that these texts involve. It is in reading and responding to the continually unsettling and challenging questions set in motion by these plays that Greek tragedy is performed and experienced.

Rush Rehm. *The Play of Space: Spatial Transformation in Greek Tragedy*. Princeton: Princeton University Press, 2002.

A searching philosophical study of the place of space, as a concept, a fact, and a form of experience, in Greek tragedy.

The distant spaces of Corinth, Delphi, the three roads, and Cithaeron each provide the setting for a memorable event in Oedipus' past. When he brings those distant events together and holds them simultaneously in his mind, the past overtakes the present and Oedipus discovers his true identity.

Literary and Language Studies

C. M. Bowra. *Sophoclean Tragedy*. Oxford: Oxford University Press, 1944.

An assessment of Sophocles as a moralist, who depends on his art to convey his moral values. An excellent introduction to the seven complete plays of Sophocles.

> It is . . . important to see what a Greek audience would feel about Oedipus' parricide and incest. For the tragic power of the play depends on the horror which these evoke. Oedipus is not legally or morally guilty of murder or of incest since he acted in ignorance. But he is something no less horrible; he is a polluted being, a man to be shunned as if he literally had some revolting and infectious plague. So far as the gods are concerned, it makes no difference whether he has acted in ignorance or not. Incest and parricide pollute him.

Francis Fergusson. *The Idea of a Theater*. Princeton: Princeton University Press, 1945.

A classic study of the rhythms that constitute the tragic drama. Fergusson lays special emphasis on the sequence of Purpose, Passion (or Suffering), and Perception (or final recognition resulting from the tragic experience).

> The element which distinguishes this theater, giving it its unique directness and depth, is the *ritual expectancy* which Sophocles assumed in his audience. . . . Sophocles' audience must have been pre-

pared . . . to consider the playing, the make-believe it was about to see—the choral invocations, with dancing and chanting; the reasoned discourses and the terrible combats of the protagonists; the mourning, the rejoicing, and the contemplation of the final stage-picture or epiphany—as imitating and celebrating the mystery of human nature and destiny. And this mystery was at once that of individual growth and development, and that of the precarious life of the human City.

S. M. Adams. *Sophocles the Playwright*. Toronto: University of Toronto Press, 1957.

Adams gives a close reading of Sophocles' plays with attention to staging issues emphasizing the interpretation of Sophocles in his own time.

Sophocles . . . gives us an Oedipus whose concern has been to escape pollution, an Oedipus who, far more than the average good man, abominates anything that has any savour of impiety and impurity; if he is also impetuous and a *tyrannos* who cannot escape the implications of that position, it is nevertheless his essential goodness that should strike us most. In what is probably its noblest form we see the contrast between man and fate.

Bernard M. W. Knox. *Oedipus at Thebes*. New Haven: Yale University Press, 1957.

A detailed study of the growth of the character of Oedipus from the *Oedipus Tyrannus* of the play represented here, to *Oedipus at Colonus,* in which Oedipus meets the culminating phase of his destiny and passes into myth.

The *Oedipus Tyrannus* of Sophocles combines two apparently irreconcilable themes, the greatness of the gods and the greatness of man, and the combination of these themes is inevitably tragic, for the greatness of the gods is most clearly and powerfully demonstrated by man's defeat. "The god is great in his laws, and he does not grow old." But man does, and not only does he grow old, he also dies. Unlike the gods, he exists in time. . . . His greatness and beauty arouse in us a pride in their magnificence which is inseparable from and increased by our sorrow over their immanent and imminent death.

G. M. Kirkwood. *A Study of Sophoclean Drama*. Ithaca: Cornell University Press, 1958.

A broad study of Sophocles' dramaturgy. Kirkwood explores the apposite view that Sophocles is a pessimist about man and his destiny and that he believes the universe is ultimately friendly to man.

The form of *Oedipus Tyrannus* has all too often been regarded as *the* Sophoclean form. Rather, it is the most perfect, and most successful; and it is the simplest. In a series of scenes, with Oedipus dominant in all, the characters, acting on each other as they grapple with the situation before them, gradually develop the life and power of the play; this life consists essentially of the nature of Oedipus as it emerges in the course of the revelations brought about by the plot.

Seth Benardete. "Sophocles' *Oedipus Tyrannus*" (1964). In Thomas Woodard, *Sophocles: A Collection of Critical Essays*. Englewood Cliffs, NJ: Prentice-Hall, 1966.

Benardete's essay on the language of *Oedipus* exposes the ironies and double entendres that anchor the action of the play.

The name of Oedipus [which means "swollen foot" in Greek] perhaps most clearly shows that the surface truth of Oedipus is the truth of his depths as well. To be crippled was considered to be a sign of tyrannical ambition and the very name of the royal family, Labdacidae, contains with it labda or lambda, the letter which resembles an uneven gait.

E. R. Dodds. "On Misunderstanding the Oedipus Rex" (1966). In Michael O'Brien, ed., *Twentieth Century Interpretations of Oedipus Rex*. Englewood Cliffs, NJ: Prentice-Hall, 1968.

A personal essay, by a well-respected British scholar, on the ultimate meaning of *Oedipus Rex*.

To me personally Oedipus is a kind of symbol of the human intelligence which cannot rest until it has solved all the riddles—even the last riddle, to which the answer is that human happiness is built on an illusion. I do not know how far Sophocles intended that. But certainly in the last lines of the play (which I firmly believe to be genuine) he does generalize the case, does appear to suggest that in some sense Oedipus is every man and every man is potentially Oedipus.

Alister Cameron. *The Identity of Oedipus the King: Five Essays on the Oedipus Tyrannus*. New York: New York University Press, 1968.

A study of the use Sophocles made of the available cultural materials to fashion a perennially cunning drama.

Oedipus' fate is, of course, not complete before the play begins. Apollo commands the search for the guilty man, commands Oedipus, knowing him well, knowing both that he is guilty and will search and therefore find himself. This Oedipus does. That is the literal record of the action. Fate is, to be sure, an ambiguous word, but not so ambiguous that we cannot recognize it here; at least if this is not a fate and its fulfillment, then I do not know what a fate can be. And yet, it remains true that Oedipus' fate by the acts he has committed is, if not complete, already in existence and indeed sealed. How can his fate be in existence and coming into existence at the same time without contradiction?

David Bain. "A Misunderstood Scene in Sophokles, Oidipous (*O.T.* 300–462)." *Greece and Rome,* October 1979. Reprinted in McAuslan and Walcott, eds., *Greek Tragedy*. Oxford: Oxford University Press, 1993.

Bain defends Oedipus from many classic interpretations, starting the "Oedipus complex" proposed by Sigmund Freud. He argues that Oedipus is stupid, as

some have called him, for not immediately calling on
the shepherd who had been a witness to Laius' murder.

Once Sophocles decided on a confrontation between
Teiresias and Oidipous early in the play, he was
inevitably faced with difficulties. The seer knows
the truth and must be forced to reveal it (otherwise
why bring him on at all?). Oidipous must not accept
what he says. By arranging his material in the way
that has been described here, Sophokles skates on
thin ice, but with a triumphant outcome. The audience is left free to concentrate on the confrontation
itself and its brilliant contrasts, on the man who sees
but does not know the truth and the blind man who
does know; on its imagery, the play on light and
darkness used literally of sight and blindness and
metaphorically of knowledge, ignorance, and the
darkness of Oidipous' acts; and finally on the psy-
chologically convincing depiction of a quarrel
between two angry men.

R. P. Winnington-Ingram. *Sophocles: An Interpretation.*
Cambridge, UK: Cambridge University Press, 1980.
Winnington-Ingram focuses on large cultural questions, including, Are the personalities of Sophocles'
characters basically intelligible to us? Can we recon-
struct, inside ourselves, the spectator mode of
Sophocles' audience?

The acts which drew down on Oedipus the wrath of
the gods were not done in pride of any kind, but in
simple ignorance. Is there then any moral in his fate?
Is there any lesson to be drawn? Yes, if it is salutary

for men to realize the fragility of human fortunes and the vast sea of ignorance in which they swim. No, if it is meant that Oedipus should have been something other than himself, without the keen energies and the thrusting intelligence which made him great; that he should have been a man like Creon, who always thinks before he speaks and then says less than he means, who is content, parasitically, to enjoy the fruits without the risks of power, a cautious man. Those who consider that Sophocles was the prophet of *sophrosyne* (prudent wisdom) should contemplate a world of Creons and wonder whether it would be any place for a tragic poet.

Charles Segal. *Tragedy and Civilization: An Interpretation of Sophocles.* Cambridge, Mass.: Harvard University Press, 1981.

An in-depth analysis of each of Sophocles' plays, focusing on the tight knit between ideas and aesthetic texture.

Oedipus' very identity conceals a dreadful violation of civilized norms, the exposure of a first child by its parents on a savage mountainside. Though the exposure of a child was permissible in classical Greece, the exposure of a firstborn son by the ruling pair of the city, not poor folk who had the excuse of poverty, is almost unprecedented. Cast out from the shelter of the house, Oedipus is made a creature of the wild, a child of the mountain and a child of Chance. He is saved from death by shepherds, men who dwell beyond the pale of the city and occupy an ambiguous position between the wild and the civilized. Thrust from his *oikos* (home), he has no name, no rooted human identity, the most basic possession of even the humblest human being.

J. Peter Euben. *The Tragedy of Political Theory: The Road Not Taken*. Princeton: Princeton University Press, 1990.

Euben discusses Greek tragedy's role in forming Greek political theory, and *Oedipus the King*'s role in the Athenian conception of the *polis* and of social action within it.

Oedipus is a traveler; like the younger sophists, he along with Jocasta questions the veracity of oracles. He is also, in his contest with Teiresias, a representative of the kind of knowledge we might call empirical, analytic, and objective. That such knowledge has its value is evidenced by Oedipus' ability to answer the Sphinx's riddle: What is four-footed in the morning, two-footed in the afternoon, and three-footed in the evening? That such knowledge is also a kind of blindness is clear from Oedipus' inability to see that as a man who requires a staff to walk he is an exception to that answer but is *the* answer to the new riddle, Who killed Laius? The abstract knowledge that enabled him to see continuity amid differences disables him from seeing the particular circumstances of his life.

P. E. Easterling. *The Cambridge Companion to Greek Tragedy*. Cambridge, UK: Cambridge University Press, 1997.

A broad study of performance, language, and art in

Greek tragedy. As in the excerpt below, it also provides a history of the *Oedipus* performances and accumulated cultural heritage.

In 1887 Sophocles' *Oedipus the King* was performed at Cambridge in the original Greek; but, despite the Cambridge precedent, a professional production of Sophocles' play was not permissible at this time in Britain. . . . Members of the British establishment were convinced, in the words of a leading actor-manager of the time, that granting a license for *Oedipus the King* might "prove injurious" and "lead to a great number of plays being written . . . appealing to a vitiated public taste solely in the cause of indecency." . . . [A] new version of the play would most probably fall foul of the censor "on the ground that it is . . . impossible to put on the stage in England a play dealing with incest."

QUESTIONS FOR DISCUSSION

It has been said that *Oedipus the King* is a mystery story, in which Oedipus is the detective searching for a criminal. Several crime novels and movies feature protagonists who search for the identity of a killer, only to discover that they are the killer. What do you think of this idea? What does it say about morality?

One of the primary debates about *Oedipus* is the role fate plays. Do you think Oedipus is a victim of fate, or does he bring his fate upon himself?

Does Oedipus' punishment seem to fit his crime of killing Laius? Is justice the point of the play? If not, what is?

What is the function of the chorus in *Oedipus the King*? Does it contribute to the development of the plot? Is the classical Greek stage especially suited to the display of choral dancing?

What do you think was the dramatic effect of the costuming—high boots, masks, stylized robes—of the actors in Greek tragedy? How would seeing the play this way affect your understanding of the action, or your feelings about it?

What is the role of Tiresias in *Oedipus the King*? Does it seem odd that he so bluntly accuses Oedipus of murder at the beginning of the play? Where does this prophet get his knowledge? Is the oracle of Apollo the source of Tiresias' wisdom?

What is the meaning of the statement, in the final passage of the chorus, that "we must call no man happy while he waits to see his last day"?

What does *Oedipus* have to say about the nature of truth? Is truth a good thing? A bad thing? How does it come to be known in the play and for the audience?

SUGGESTIONS FOR THE
INTERESTED READER

If you enjoyed *Oedipus the King*, you might also be interested in the following:

Mythology by Edith Hamilton. A great resource for figuring out all the backstories Sophocles' audience would have known, including the various behaviors of the gods, and Creon and Oedipus' extended family.

Medea by Euripedes. Not fully appreciated in his own time, Euripedes is now seen as both the inheritor of Sophocles' genius and a vital innovator of his tradition. Many of Euripedes' plays, including his comedies, are still performed today, including this one. *Medea* is the tragic story of the hero Jason's foreign wife, who, spurned by him, commits a terrible act of revenge.

Oedipus Rex directed by Julie Taymor. A lavishly staged, 1992 made-for-TV version of Igor Stravinsky's opera version of the play, with a libretto by Jean Cocteau, sculpture and masks by Julie Taymor, and a chorus performed by the Japanese Saito Kenen Festival dancers.

Lone Star (DVD, VHS). Called "Oedipus Tex" by some reviewers, this acclaimed 1996 film written and directed by John Sayles explores the explosive secrets of a little Texas town and its legendary sheriff, Buddy Deeds. Buddy's son has followed, somewhat unwillingly, in his father's footsteps as sheriff and explores the suspicious cover-up of a decades-old murder in which his father might have been involved. The film stars Chris Cooper, Matthew McConaughey, and Kris Kristofferson.

Not sure what to read next?

Visit Pocket Books online at
www.SimonSays.com

**Reading suggestions for
you and your reading group**

New release news
Author appearances
Online chats with your favorite writers
Special offers
And much, much more!

10421

BESTSELLING ENRICHED CLASSICS